P9-DJV-562

eleven and holding

eleven and holding

MARY PENNEY

HARPER
An Imprint of HarperCollinsPublishers

Eleven and Holding
Copyright © 2016 by Mary Penney
All rights reserved. Printed in the United States of America.
No part of this book may be used or reproduced in any manner
whatsoever without written permission except in the case of brief
quotations embodied in critical articles and reviews. For information
address HarperCollins Children's Books, a division of HarperCollins
Publishers, 195 Broadway, New York, NY 10007.
www.harpercollinschildrens.com

Library of Congress Control Number: 2015951377
ISBN 978-0-06-240547-0 (trade bdg.)

16 17 18 19 20   PC/RRDH   10 9 8 7 6 5 4 3 2 1
❖
First Edition

For my beautiful, gifted, and generous soul sister,
Robin LaFevers,
who has always carried the Chap Stick for us.

CHAPTER ONE

It was a steaming, hot summer day, and I was camped out in front of my former life, just watching and waiting to steal it back somehow. The sidewalk burned under me like a griddle, as it had for the thousand other Saturday mornings I'd spent sitting on this very spot—the corner of Broad and Alameda Streets in Constant, Colorado. You might think that a place named Constant would be famous for things always staying the same. You'd be dead wrong. The only thing constant about this place was how fast things could change.

I felt for the folded bus ticket in my back pocket, making sure it was still there.

And half hoped it wasn't.

I studied the handprints etched in the cement next

* * * * *

to me—Nana, Dad, Mom, and me. The family I used to have before everything got messed up. Before Nana died. Before Dad went to fight in Iraq. Before nearly everything that was good about my family changed.

I traced a finger around my kid palm print. Even when I was only five, my hands had been big. Six years later I'm the one opening all the jars in my house.

I sucked down the rest of my iced latte and elbowed my best friend. "Twee, go get me a refill. But just milk, whipped cream, and a shot of chocolate— no espresso." I nudged my cup at her. "Don't tell *him* it's for me."

Twee elbowed me back, harder. "You go," she said, not looking up from the book cradled in her arms.

I set my cup down with a sigh and then studied the scab on my knee. Playing soccer on blacktop was never a good idea. Lifting an end of the scab, I peered underneath to see if it was ready to come off.

"Ew. Macy, leave that alone, will you?" Twee swiped long, dark bangs out of her eyes and glanced back toward the shop door. "Aren't you *ever* going to go in again? It's been—" She turned my wrist to look at my watch.

"A year, ten months, and twelve days," I muttered.

Twee knew it was hard enough for me to look at Caffeine Nana's, let alone go inside. But even without turning around, I could see every brick in the place—the giant front window I'd washed a million times, and the green stools at the counter that you could spin to nearly warp speed. It was completely the same as it had always been, but totally different.

Still, I sat out in front of it every Saturday. The dirty rat fink who bought the place always gave us free drinks. But I hoped to God he'd one day choke on a big, foamy wad of guilt.

Twee read my face, then shrugged. "All righty then." She smacked my hand away from my scab again. "I'll be back. Hold my seat." She jumped up and sprinted toward the café door.

I glanced down at the book she'd left. It was one of her five-pound volumes on Vietnam. She devoured them like some kind of junkie. Twee had been born in Vietnam and was adopted out. Her name was spelled T-U-I, but when she started school, everyone—even the teachers—were calling her "Too-ey" by mistake, so her folks changed it to Twee to make it easier. She'd lived in Constant since she was three months old, but I think part of her soul got left behind in Da Nang.

We called her adoptive parents Mr. and Mrs. Melting Pot, because they had seven kids, each adopted from a different country. And now Mrs. Pot was pregnant with twins, due any day.

Twins! Poor Twee. Babies were totally overrated. And I was an expert on the subject. I'd just spent my entire summer taking care of my baby brother, Jack, aka Drool Master J. Now that he'd started walking, he was pretty much a wrecking crew in a diaper.

It was my own fault. I never should have encouraged him to stand up.

Soon Twee would have *two* drool masters running loose in the house. Plus, she was the nicest kid in her family, so we already knew who was going to end up doing all the babysitting.

Around adults, Twee would politely say that she was "superexcited" about the babies, but I think it was the kind of excited we felt about me starting middle school next week.

As in not. At all. Since Twee was a year younger than me, she was only going into sixth grade, and I was headed off to Kit Carson Middle School. Not only did I have to change buildings, I would be in classes without my best friend. We swore we wouldn't let it change anything, and we'd spend all our outside time together. But I was used to seeing her all day, nearly every day. It just wouldn't be the same.

I'd begged Mom to let me repeat sixth grade, so Twee and I wouldn't be split up. It wouldn't be so bad. I'd had most all the teachers, could find my way around blindfolded, and I knew to pack my lunch on Thursdays when the cafeteria served shepherd's pie. But Mom wouldn't go for it. She was always encouraging me to make new friends. She loved Twee like a second daughter, but she thought we both needed to "branch out." We thought we were just fine the way we were. We, at least, were a constant.

Mom took me to Kit Carson for a visit last month—a crack at getting me "in the mood." Stucco faced. One floor. Brand-new. And it smelled more like a hospital or a science lab than like kids. It would take years before that place would get broken in. And the trees outside were still runts held up by sticks. What kind of school had no shade? They'd torn the old middle school down when it was still perfectly good in my opinion. It had two stories, was made of red brick, and had giant columns out front.

It had heft. It had character. My nana had gone there, and so had my dad and aunt Liv. Now I was stuck going to the butt-ugliest school you ever saw.

But this battle was not over by any means. If they wouldn't hold me back a grade, I'd get *sent* back. All I had to do was push the right buttons. . . .

The ground under me vibrated, and I looked up from Twee's book. It sounded like one of those big sit-down lawn mowers was headed down Broad. I shaded my eyes with my hand, and I tried to make it out. The sun blazed off its chrome, blinding me. It was too small for a car but too big for a motorcycle.

I stood up for a better look—just in time to get slammed from behind. "WHHAAA!" I landed hard on my hip. I swore with a word that would have cost me a week's allowance in the cuss jar at home.

Switch threw me a smile from the back of his skateboard. He shouted over the music blasting from his earbuds. "Hey— Sorry!"

"Learn to ride that thing!" I shouted back.

As if he needed to. Switch was the slickest skater around—almost a legend, even though he was only fourteen. I'd hated his guts since he'd thrown water balloons at a Veterans Day parade float—the one my dad was riding. As if he'd heard me, Switch turned again, skimming the narrow sidewalk ledge. He raised his lips in a kiss.

And not like a romantic one—more like "kiss my you-know-what."

The rumbling machine roared up then, framing him in my view. It *was* a motorcycle, a humongous one, with a sidecar, and it was headed in Switch's direction. I saw the accident even before it happened. I tried to yell a warning.

Switch kick-flipped off the sidewalk, and his foot

caught the corner of his board. It shot out from under him like a torpedo. He rolled onto the street, straight into the motorcycle's path.

The bike veered sharply and cut up onto the sidewalk. Right toward Twee, who had just backed out of the café balancing two cups in her hands and a big muffin under her chin.

"LOOOOK OUT!" I screamed.

Her head snapped around. She froze. The motorcycle crashed inches from her feet. The sidecar slammed smack into the front window.

The glass shattered and fell like an ice storm. We stood spellbound to the last tinkle.

The driver jumped off the motorbike. "Oh, GOD! Oh my GOD! Are you all *right*?" He tore off his helmet. Only he wasn't a he, he was a she. And she had two long gray braids.

Twee dropped both cups now, like she'd forgotten to before. She jumped back as the milky lava hit her flip-flops.

The café door flew open, and Chuck rushed out. "What happened? Is everyone okay?" He looked wild, and his sneakers slid and screeched on the glass. "Macy? Twee?" His face was tight with panic. He stared at the old woman next to Twee. "Ginger!" he exploded.

I gently pulled Twee away from all the glass and spillage. She was still in slow-mo.

The woman called Ginger tried to smooth the hair out of her face with fingers that shook. "Chuck, I'm so sorry!" She gestured toward the window and then pressed her fingers over her lips. "Look what I've done!" Then she looked at us. "Thank God none of these kids got hurt— I could have— Oh my God, I could have never forgiven myself."

Chuck blew out a breath that could have inflated a small wading pool. He started to speak and then stopped and just looked at us.

I looked away.

"What the heck happened, Ginger? And *now* will you *finally* get rid of this thing?" He ripped the keys from the ignition. "You're not driving this home."

She swiped them back just as quickly. "I'll be fine!"

"Hey— It's not her fault!" I pushed my way in between the two of them. "She had to swerve so she wouldn't hit that idiot!" I said, waving toward the street.

"What idiot?" Chuck asked, looking around.

Switch was nowhere to be found.

"He's gone," I said, disgusted. "He rode off and he's *fine*." I turned my back to Chuck and pulled

Twee over to one of the outdoor tables and sat her down. "Hey. You sure you're okay?"

"Yeah, yeah. Just . . . wow. That was intense."

Customers from inside the café stepped out to check out the damage. "Watch the glass, everyone!" Chuck said. "Careful now! I'll go get a broom." He put an arm across Ginger's shoulders and gave her a squeeze. "Why don't you come in a second."

"Don't fuss. I'm fine." She stepped away from his arm. "Go get the broom, and I'll sweep up."

"You need to sit down. I'll fix you some tea." He picked up the cups Twee had dropped and stepped around the puddles. He came over and put his hand on Twee's shoulder. "And you're sure you're all right? Can I get you anything?"

She shook her head, still a little shell-shocked.

I glared at his hand on Twee's shoulder until he removed it.

"Refills, you two?" he asked.

"No thank you," I said coldly.

"Well, if you change your mind—" He turned at the door. He was still white as a ghost. "Ginger, I mean it. Come take a load off, okay?"

"In a minute," she said.

After he left I went and crouched over the mound of broken glass, sifting through the pieces. Careful as I was, a bright bulb of blood popped out on my thumb. I sucked it up and kept looking.

Ginger's braids swung into my vision. "Honey, Chuck and I can clean this up."

Twee came and squatted next to me. "Macy, what are you doing?"

When I didn't answer, Twee started talking to Ginger like I wasn't there. "Her grandma owned this place for, like, thirty years."

"Thirty-seven," I corrected, under my breath.

"Yeah, thirty-seven. And it used to be called just Nana's, but when Chuck bought it from their family—"

"Stole it," I clarified, wondering if she was going to share my family's entire history or just the highlights.

Twee rolled her eyes and went on. "He renamed it Caffeine Nana's." She stopped as Chuck came back out with a broom, a dustpan, and a big plastic trash can.

"Macy, please," he said, seeing me bent over the glass. "I'll clean it up. I don't want you to cut yourself."

I tucked my bloody thumb into my fist. "I'm not cleaning. I'm looking for something."

He stared at me a moment, like he was going to say something, but then changed his mind. He steered Ginger's motorbike away from the window.

Twee tried to act like a major cold front hadn't just blown in. "So, anyway," she said to the woman. "I'm Twee, and this is Macy." She patted my hindquarters.

"Ginger," she said. "Ginger Grady." She reached across me and shook Twee's hand. Then she gave me a handkerchief for my thumb, which continued to bleed.

I finally found the piece I wanted and eased it out of the pile. I looked up at Ginger. "Can I keep your handkerchief until I get home? I could mail it back to you."

"No need for that. It's yours. Careful now, though."

Twee and Ginger watched in silence as I bundled up the glass and then slipped it into my backpack, safely between two books. I looked up at the sky, which was getting dark and ready for its summer afternoon downpour. I checked my watch. "We better go, Twee, or we're going to miss the matinee." I felt my front pocket for my movie money. "S'nice meeting you, Ginger," I said, mostly to be polite.

The wind kicked up, and what looked like a flock of white birds flew out of a bag sitting in the sidecar of Ginger's motorcycle.

"Uh-oh, your papers!" Twee hurried after the sheets that swirled down the sidewalk.

Ginger pounced on the remaining sheets in the

bag, calling out to Twee, "Don't worry about them! I have more."

She turned to me and held out a hand. "It's been a pleasure to meet you, Macy. Perhaps I'll see you again sometime." She paused and considered me a moment. "I hope so."

I put out my nonbleeding hand, awkward like. I never had gotten the hang of shaking hands, especially with adults. But her grip was warm, like she was handing me something nice. I took a moment to study her. She had a good face, strong and open. I liked that she didn't try to cover all her wrinkles with a bunch of beige makeup. Her eyes were bright green, not brownish green like mine, and I got the feeling she didn't miss much.

Just then, I had a flash of her sitting alone, real sad. I shook off the prickling that ran between my shoulder blades. Dad used to say that meant someone had just walked over your grave. Only in this case, it didn't feel like my grave. It felt like someone else's. It creeped me out.

"Five hundred bucks!" Twee whistled as she came up beside us, looking down at the papers she'd rescued. She cut herself short, embarrassed, and held the stack out to Ginger. "I'm really sorry about your dog. But maybe you've already found him?" she asked, hopeful.

Ginger glanced at the front of the flyer, and I watched pain creep across her face and settle into familiar folds. "No, my sweet boy, he's still gone," she said.

"You should post—" Twee started. And then like we'd rehearsed it, we all looked at the giant jagged hole that used to be the shop's front window—where you used to be able to put up flyers and posters. Seeing Nana's window busted out like that made me hollow inside. Like someone had taken a melon baller and scooped out my internal organs. The way I felt the day of her funeral. And the way I felt whenever I look at the calendar and count how many months Dad has been gone this time.

"Guess you can't put one here," Twee said. "But you can put some up inside! I'm sure Chuck won't mind. I can take a couple in for you. Oh! But you're going to go have tea with him, right?"

Ginger shook her head, "Oh, no. I'm not going in." As in, no way was she going inside.

Huh, I thought. *A woman after my own heart. She must know what a crook Chuck is too.*

"Do you want to give me a few?" Twee asked. "I can help post some around town."

"Sure, that would be lovely. But don't post any here—all right, honey?"

Wow. Her distaste for Chuck was strong. Now, she was really growing on me. She didn't even want her missing-dog poster crossing over his threshhold.

"Uh, okay," Twee said, puzzled. She thrust them at me to hold and helped Ginger back on her bike. I lifted a hand and waved as she gunned her motor.

I tried not to look at the flyers. With just one week left of summer, I had no time for a missing dog and sad old woman. But Twee had a heart the size of an army tank and was the patron saint of hopeless causes. She once dragged a homeless man to school for her social studies project. I had to keep a close eye on her.

After all, I had a missing father, and that trumped everything. It wasn't like he was still in the service. He *could* come home, but he hadn't. And I was pretty sure I knew why.

I put the flyers behind my back, rolling them into a tube, chewing the inside of my cheek. *C'mon, Twee, hurry up!* She had climbed into the sidecar and was grinning up at Ginger. I recognized the look. She was in Serious Infatuation Mode.

Twee and I loved so many of the same things, we could nearly read each other's minds. But we had one big giant difference. I liked my world nice and predictable. Every Saturday, after we hang out in front of Caffeine Nana's awhile, Twee and I go to the movies; sit in the fourth row, left side; and I always eat a jumbo bag of Red Vines. Twee, on the other hand, would just as soon throw our regular Saturday plans to the wind and go riding off on this woman's motorcycle.

Or spend our entire day combing the streets for Ginger's dog. I sighed and dug around for my patience.

Lord, it was hot. I'd kill for a glass of lemonade. I tried not to think about the big, frosty pitchers that Nana used to keep in the giant steel fridge in back. I fanned at my face with the flyers, and the headline swept back and forth like a squeaky windshield wiper. "Have You Seen Mr. McDougall? Have You Seen Mr. McDougall?" I tried to ignore the picture, but it felt like it was staring at me. I gave up and took a long look. In the photo, Mr. McDougall, I presumed, was sitting in the motorbike's sidecar with a toothy dog smile and a bubble-gum pink tongue. He looked like some kind of white Labrador. If Mom would ever let me have a dog, I'd probably want one like this, or maybe a big old hound dog. I took a big breath. *Sorry, Mr. McWhatever. I hope you find your way home soon, but I'm not your girl. I can't help you. I've got my hands full with a missing party of my own.*

There was nothing I could do to bring back my nana, but I wasn't going to stand by and watch the rest of my family fall to pieces. I was Montgomery "Gum" Hollinquest's daughter, after all. We didn't give up. We were fighters.

I just had to find him, so I could remind him of that fact.

Dear Mr. Jimenez,

I got your letter welcoming me to your seventh-grade homeroom. I haven't ever gotten a letter from a teacher in the mail before. And I've never had a man teacher before.

You said all your new seventh-grade students should write back and share seven things about ourselves. You said it could be something interesting, unique, or funny. When you shared seven things about yourself in the letter, you said you once fell off a camel in Egypt. And broke your tailbone! I didn't know if that was supposed to be funny or interesting. Anyway,

The First Thing About Me: my best friend, Twee, is not coming with me to Kit Carson Middle School because she's only going into sixth grade. She didn't flunk or anything like that. See, Twee is one year younger than me, so we are in different grades. But we're not used to being apart. I'm telling you now, so you won't think I don't have any friends when you see me sitting alone in the cafeteria sometimes, which, really, let's be honest, will be all the time.

I have a feeling I am going to have a hard time in seventh grade. I already have nearly forgotten everything I learned in sixth! You shouldn't feel bad if you want to flunk me—even during the first week of school. I'm not the kind of student that would hold that against you. And if I stayed back a year, Twee could help me with algebra. I am terrible at finding y.

Yours very sincerely,

Macy L. Hollinquest

17

CHAPTER TWO

"No!" I nearly shouted as Twee came toward me, her eyes glazed. They get like that when she thinks she has the best idea ever.

"'No' in every language of the universe. *Ni, non, votch', nem,* Nein, N-O!"

"Macy, come on! It's five hundred dollars! We've got a whole week left before school starts. Just think of what we could do with all that money. It's a fortune!"

I pressed the flyers at her. "Here, *you* put these up. You told her you would. Keep *me* out of it."

"But don't you want to help her?"

Silent glare from my end.

"But she's so nice," she added, trying another tack. "Don't you think she's nice, Macy?"

I headed down the street, walking fast. Twee

* * * * *

followed, hot on my tracks.

"Sure. Other than nearly killing you on that death mobile of hers, she's a peach. But I don't have time."

"What do you mean you don't have time? Your mom promised if you babysat Jack all summer, you could have this last week of summer to do what you want to do."

"I mean I have other plans already, and they don't include looking for a lost dog. If you want to, go right ahead."

Behind me, Twee fell silent a long moment—too long. That should have tipped me right off. She yanked the bus ticket from my back pocket. I turned to grab it from her, but she'd always been a little taller, and stronger, than I was. She held me off.

"What *is* this—a round-trip ticket to Los Robles? One child's fare?" She looked at me like she'd just found plans in my pocket to hack into the Pentagon's computers.

I swiped at the ticket again, a hot flush steaming up my neck. She held it over her head, taking full advantage of the 2.75 inches she had on me.

"Who's this for? *You* do not ride buses."

Technically, this was true. Not since kindergarten. After some pretty spectacular projectile vomiting, the PTA encouraged my mother to find me other transportation. At the start of every new school year, though, Mom would pack me up with a good-sized barf bag and have me try it again. It never changes. Buses and me don't mix.

I dug my fingers into both sides of Twee's shorts. "Unless you want to moon all the old guys in Hadley's Barbershop right now, you better give me my ticket!"

Twee grabbed her waistband and held on, still holding the ticket high. "Who's it for? Just tell me!"

I pulled, and her shorts dipped dangerously low on her nonexistent hips. "Give it, Twee—*now*—or here comes the great Continental Divide." My voice was hard as baked clay.

"All right! All right already! If you're going to have a stroke about it!" She yanked her shorts back up and handed the ticket to me. "Here, take it. Don't tell me anything. I could give a flip."

Folding the ticket into quarters, I crammed it back into my pocket. I crossed my arms tight against my chest while I caught up with my breath. I studied my new crop of arm freckles while I considered what I could safely tell her. "Okay. It's for me. I'm taking the bus to Los Robles to get some school clothes," I lied.

Twee's eyebrows shot up. "Well, this gets weirder by the minute. Number one, you would rather swim in stew than ride a bus. And number two. . . ." She paused. "Well, number two, you hate shopping." She narrowed her eyes. "Give it. What's going on, Macy?"

My eyes fixed on the gap between her two front teeth, while I calculated the risk. "All right. Look, I'm going to see my dad. But no one can know about it! Especially not my mom. This has got to be completely secret."

She opened her mouth and then snapped it shut. "Okay, but I'm going with you. You are not taking the bus to Los Robles all by yourself. The ticket's for August thirtieth, right?" She cocked her head. "Wednesday?"

There was no way I could take her with me. I would trust Twee with my life, but with things that fell in the category of Stuff Guaranteed to Send a Parent to an Early Grave, Twee was a lightweight. Not to mention the fact that for some reason, she didn't like my dad anymore. Which I never could understand or even get her to admit. But it was absolutely true. She'd go into this polite-but-chilly routine when he was around. I definitely didn't need any of that in the vicinity while I was trying to convince him to come home.

"The ticket says the thirtieth, but that isn't actually the date I'm going," I fibbed. "They have this Labor Day special. It starts on the thirtieth, but it's good for Wednesday, Thursday, or Friday. I'm going on Thursday."

Twee's face scrunched, trying to follow all this. "They put your real departure date in the computer," I explained. Lame, but it seemed to work.

She turned my arm to look at my watch. I was the designated timekeeper. Her job was to always carry the Chap Stick. "Maybe we should go by the bus station before the movie and get my ticket, then. I don't want them to sell out."

I grabbed her sleeve and hustled her down toward the movie theater. "No time! We're already late. I'll get it for you Monday. My treat! I really appreciate you going with me. But bring goggles and a raincoat."

"Because we are actually taking a submarine to Los Robles?" she asked, looking confused.

"No—because I may be barfing on you the whole trip. Just remember. You wanted to go!"

"Shoot, Macy. What's a little barf between best friends?"

I tried not to think about how long she would be mad at me after she discovered that I had gone to Los Robles without her. Because if it brought my dad home, it'd be worth every lousy bit of it.

The wood floor under my bed felt cool against my belly as I wiggled my way to the middle. I gently unwrapped the piece of glass I'd saved from Nana's window, careful not to cut myself again. It was the original window's glass from when Nana first opened the coffee shop almost forty years ago. That window had never been broken—until today. It was a very bad omen.

Every spring Nana would have the window painter come and redo it. Never change it, just repaint the loopy gold letters. When Chuck stole the café from us, he'd added *"caffeine"* in front of Nana's name when the painter came. I think he thought it made the shop seem hipper. I thought it was just dumber.

Thankfully, he'd kept the rest of the window the same. Across the bottom, it had always read:

GOOD COFFEE, GOOD TIMES, GOOD LORD, COME ON IN
SERVING IT UP BY THE CUPFUL SINCE 1977

The piece of glass I had saved just read "good tim." The *es* hadn't survived the crash.

I rewrapped it in an old undershirt and unhooked the bungee cord that strapped a big, long, thin box to the underside of my mattress frame. When your mom is a snoopy probation officer, you have to be very smart about where you hide your private things. I knew for a fact she couldn't get under my bed. I'd watched her try a couple of months ago to drag Jack out. It wasn't because she was fat or anything, but she was kind of stacked.

I was hoping to get my future boobs from my dad's side of the family, where they came in smaller sets.

Next to my private box, my old Cookie Monster puppet hung from the bed slats. He was my version of a scarecrow. I had to put him up to keep Jack from going under my bed. I didn't want him *ever* getting into my box. And to Jack, the Cookie Monster was the devil incarnate.

The familiar smell of my life history greeted me as I pulled the lid off. An old cigarette butt of Nana's rolled around the bottom. The end still had her lipstick marks on it. She wore one lipstick—an orangey color called Sweet Sunset, and it never changed. Nana loved to smoke, and in the end it killed her.

My grandpa had died before I was born. Whenever I asked about him, everyone got kind of quiet. Especially Dad and his big sister, my aunt Liv. Guess Grandpa hadn't been the greatest father ever. When I was real little I'd heard Aunt Liv tell one of her friends that he'd drunk himself to death. That worried me, because I'd been trying for some time to see if I could drink up all my bathwater. I liked the taste of it, and it seemed it would be a great accomplishment for a kid. I gave up trying after that.

I figured out when I was older that they meant he drank too much booze.

I put Nana's cigarette butt between my lips and let it hang like she did when she was working on her accounts. She once told me she'd come back and haunt me if I ever started smoking, but since it wasn't lit, I'm sure it didn't count.

I poked at Jack's belly-button stump that I had sealed up in a Ziploc bag. No one knew I'd saved it. When he was older, I was going to sneak in some night while he was sleeping and glue it back on him. Then I'd try to convince him it had grown back. It would completely freak him out. God, I couldn't wait.

I peeled the cigarette off my lip where it had started to stick and pulled out Dad's letter. It had come about three weeks ago. I was home babysitting Jack the day it arrived. Mom didn't know about it.

He had been gone for close to seven months now. When he first got out of the army, I thought he'd finally be home all the time. I'd been dreaming of having a regular family for so, *so* long. It wasn't bad when it was just me and Mom at home waiting for him. But after Jack was born, it seemed Mom never gave me a thought unless she needed someone to help her. I didn't want to be her staff. I missed just being the kid.

Not that I didn't love my little brother—it just changed everything when he came.

I held Dad's letter to my nose, trying to find his smell—shaving cream, and the cigars he always tried to hide from my mom. But it just smelled like mail. I had been surprised to get a letter, direct to me, from my dad. But I guess it was the only way to keep Mom from reading it. He probably figured she wouldn't open a letter that had my name on it. Plus, he had sent me something in the envelope besides the letter.

The return address might as well have been written in hieroglyphics. My dad had extremely messy handwriting. Like if you gave a whole pot of coffee to a monkey and then handed him a leaky pen. But I had gotten pretty good at decoding Dad's scribble. I was even better at it than my mom. When he'd first gone overseas, we sent him with a supply of envelopes that were already made out to us. Just in case email was down, which he said happened a lot over in Iraq.

Dear Short Stack,

Just a quick note so I can return this money I borrowed from you last time I was home. Not a bad interest rate, huh? Doubled your money! Remember our deal not to tell Mom, okay? If she knew I'd lost my wallet again, she'd be really sore at me.

I miss you and Jack like the dickens. My new assignment is great—wish I could tell you more about it, but that's the Department of Defense for you—their special projects are very hush-hush. I have to stay with it to the end. So, it doesn't look like I'll be able to get home for your birthday like we planned. I can't believe my baby girl is going to be twelve! But I promise you we'll celebrate as soon as I can get finished here.

Until then, mind your mom, kiss Jack, and leave the porch light on for me. I see your face everywhere, Macy—even in the stars.

All my love,

Dad

This was just so wrong. I had to find him. I had to convince him to come home for my birthday. Sometimes he called my birthday our anniversary. He said it was the "anniversary of us," since it marked how many years we'd been a father and daughter.

How was I supposed to turn twelve without him here? Twelve was a huge deal. It was *the last official year of being a kid.* I might even get my period! And boobs! And sweat glands!

In all the years my dad had been in the army, he'd only missed one birthday, and that was because he was fighting in Iraq. I tried to celebrate it without him, but it wasn't the same. I crashed the new bike

Mom had gotten me, broke my arm, and chipped my tooth. And our freezer died, and all my birthday dessert melted into a big, rainbow sherbet puddle. Which is not as pretty as it sounds. After that, Dad promised me he'd never miss another one so long as he lived. And now . . . well, now what?

It wasn't just me that needed him home either. The longer he was gone, the smaller the empty space next to my mom got. Ever since the café got sold and Dad took off, it seemed like the only thing that mattered to her was Little Lord Jack, and her job. Even worse, *Chuck* had been calling her a lot lately, supposedly asking her questions about the business. If that were true, I don't know why my mom always giggled so much. There's nothing funny about coffee.

I wasn't about to take any of this sitting down. I was Gum's daughter after all, and Nana's "best girl." I owed it to both of them to get this family back on track, back to the way it used to be. Back to the way it was *supposed* to be.

Even if I had to do it all by myself.

Twee pounded up the stairs behind me and dropped her overnight bag on the floor of my bedroom with a thud. She kicked off her shoes and flung herself down on the bed next to mine. We spent nights together so often my mom bought Twee her own permanent guest bed for my room. I didn't spend the night as often at Twee's because there were already so many kids over there, it was like a kid zoo.

"I am so full! Your mom is such a good cook. I'd weigh a ton and a half if I lived here." She sucked at the ends of her fingers like a Hoover, in case she'd missed any pizza sauce. "My dad cooked tonight because Mom is about to explode with babies. Her doctor told her to stay in bed for the next few days. It looks like a mountain has fallen on her and pinned her to the bed. Anyway, he was making tofu and kale tacos," she said, with a disgusted look. She rolled over onto her stomach and rummaged through her bag on the floor. "I brought you something!" She pulled out a squashed paper bag with a ribbon tied around the top. "Here! Open it!"

"What's this for? It's not my birthday yet," I asked, suspicious. I didn't want any birthday presents or any celebrating until Dad was back. It would be a big, fat jinx if I did.

"Well, it nearly is. But this isn't for your birthday. It's for starting middle school. Open it!" she said, pushing it into my lap.

I pulled off the ribbon and looked inside. I poked

through the contents with one finger. Like it might detonate.

Twee squirmed next to me and then apparently couldn't take the wait anymore. She grabbed the bag and dumped it over the bed. "Ta-*da!*"

I surveyed the pile. "Makeup? You bought me *makeup?*"

"It's just lip gloss and stuff. Oh! And look. I got you some Hello Kitty tweezers. Let's pluck your eyebrows. I read in a magazine that you have to do that first, so your eyes really pop."

She came at me with the hot-pink metal instrument. I ducked away. "I like my eyebrows! And I don't want my eyes to pop—"

"But your brows are furry."

I smoothed the right one in place. "They look just like my dad's."

"My point exactly. Nobody wants *dad* eyebrows, Macy."

"Maybe I do—"

"Let me just get a few of the big, long ones," she said, lunging for me with Hello Kitty's pointy end.

I swatted her away. "Cut it out!"

She stopped midattack and glared at me. Then dropped the tweezers. "Fine! But you're doing lip gloss. I spent all my allowance on this stuff. It is *not* going to waste." She peeled off its protective covering and then pulled out a long, sticky-looking wand. It smelled extremely raspberry. "Now, close your mouth."

I shrugged in surrender and pressed my lips closed.

"Well, now your lips have completely disappeared. Not so tight, Mace—poof 'em back up."

"For Pete's sake!" I grumbled, and grabbed the wand from her. I swiped it around my mouth a few times.

"Wait— It's not like Chap Stick! You have to stay inside the lines."

My lips felt heavy and . . . adhesive. Like I'd just pressed my mouth into Pooh's honeypot.

Twee hooted. "You have it ALL over. Let me go get you a tissue. And a mirror! We're going to start over."

"Look, I really appreciate the presents, but I don't see why I have to wear this stuff."

"You don't have to, but all the other girls will be. Don't you want to fit in?"

I shrugged again. Fitting in wasn't something I'd ever had to worry about. Twee and I had each other and didn't worry so much about anyone else.

Twee's forehead frowned. "Listen, kids in middle

school are different from the kids in elementary," she said. "I've watched my sisters go through it. You don't want to stand out too much or you'll get picked on."

"They're going to pick on me for having eyebrows?"

"Well, that, and you sort of throw your clothes together like it doesn't matter how they look. And sometimes it looks like they came out of the hamper."

"Well, duh! Sometimes my mom puts things in the hamper that are still perfectly good to wear. And I don't care how they look. I only care how they feel. I like things soft and not all stiffy and—"

"I know, Macy! And I'm trying to tell you, you can get away with that in elementary school, but in *middle* school, you have to pay more attention to how you dress."

"Says who?" I grumbled again. "It's not like I'm trying to get a boyfriend or anything. I just want to survive the year until you get there."

"Hold still!" Twee said as she tried to wipe the extra lip gloss off my mouth.

I swiped the tissue from her and scrubbed it all from my lips.

"Macy— Stop! It looked really nice on you. Least the parts where it was on your lips."

"Maybe, but I bet when you try to eat a sandwich, all the crumbs stick to you afterward. For like days, probably. You want me to sit in the cafeteria at Kit Carson with my lunch glued to my lips?"

Twee gave me a playful swat, but then her look got serious. "I hate it that I won't be there with you."

"I know." I sighed long and hard. "But if anyone makes fun of my eyebrows or wrinkled clothes, I'll get their address, and you can go whoop them after school. Deal?"

Mom stuck her head in the doorway just then, and we both jumped. I swear that woman could sneak up on the Secret Service.

"Sorry, girls! I didn't mean to interrupt." She barged in anyway, and turned on the overhead light. It completely irritated me. Like nearly everything else she'd done this summer had. Aunt Liv said it was early teenage hormones. All I knew was that Mom had turned into squeaky chalk. Sometimes I wondered how I'd survive almost seven more years at home. Then there were times I'd still want to just crawl up in her lap and have her rub my neck like she used to.

I wiped my mouth against my sleeve for good measure and left a purple stripe. Not that she'd care if I wore lip gloss. I just didn't want her making a big deal about it.

"S'kay, Mrs. Hollinquest. You weren't interrupting," Twee said.

"I just wondered if you girls wanted to come help me crush the cookies for our ice cream sundaes. Our little man down there is pining for you. He keeps pointing at the stairs and mooing."

"That's only because you keep laughing when he does it," I said, raining on her sunny little parade.

She gave me a look, letting me know she didn't like my tone.

My mom had girl eyebrows, I noticed, skinny ones with an arch in the middle. I didn't look anything like her. She was tall and thin everywhere except her chest and never stopped moving. I was not tall—least not yet, and I moved strictly when I needed to.

"We'll be down in a sec," I said, trying not to sound completely snotty.

Mom backed out the door with a wave, and broke back in a moment later. "Macy, that reminds me! Could you watch Jack for me on Wednesday?"

I looked at her like she'd just asked me to give her my bone marrow and a few molars.

She held her hands up. "I know! I *know* I said you could have the whole week off, but Katie called this afternoon, and she can't sit on Wednesday. And I've got juvenile court all day."

I shook my head back and forth so hard it almost

spun all the way around. My ticket to Los Robles was for Wednesday.

"Please, Mace—I'll make it up to you. I'm in a real jam here. How about if I pay you time and a half?"

I kept shaking my head. No way.

She wheedled on. "I'll treat you and Twee to dinner at Galaxy Burger and a movie. Better yet, I'll stay home and let you two go without me. Please? What do you say?"

My mind raced around my life, trying to hold it all together. Monday I had soccer tryouts, which I absolutely couldn't miss. Dad had really wanted me to play this year. Tuesday I promised Aunt Liv I'd go over to help her crate her cat, who was totally mental. She needed to take her to the vet. Thursday, the express bus to Los Robles didn't run at all, and Friday, the southbound bus didn't come back until after midnight. And my curfew was nine p.m. I had to go Wednesday.

"I'll babysit for Jack," Twee volunteered.

"You will?" I turned to look at her, and a big yellow caution sign flashed in my mind.

"Sure, no sweat." She gave me a squeeze around the shoulders and vaulted off the bed toward my mother. "I'd do anything for Macy, just like I *know* she'd do anything for me." She turned and gave me

35

an evil grin. She pulled a white folded square out of her hoodie pocket and tossed it over to me as she left.

It landed in my lap. I didn't even need to open it, because I knew exactly what it was. It was that lost-dog flyer. I smelled blackmail.

CHAPTER THREE

My teeth banged together as I bumped my mountain bike up the curb in front of 173 Pomegranate Lane and eased off the saddle. I sucked lukewarm mango juice from my water bottle. Twee rode up behind me, scraping her pedal along the curb, a grating sound that made me wince.

I grabbed her handlebars, stopping her. "Twee! Use your brakes, will you?"

She nodded, panting, and took a big slug of water from her bottle. "This it?" she asked, looking at the neat, white cottage in front of us.

Nodding, I pointed at the bright polished address numbers, almost hidden by a jungle of wild purple vines near the front door. The whole yard looked like an army of green thumbs had launched an attack. My

* * * *

mom would go nuts for this place.

"Look," I said, unbuckling my helmet. "Since you've blackmailed me into helping you, I will, but don't get your hopes up. Dogs are pretty smart, and most don't get lost. They get run over or stolen."

Twee swung her leg over her bike and wheeled it toward the front of the house, ignoring me.

I picked up my bike and followed her. "Hey, don't get bent. I just don't think it's going to be as easy as walking around the block calling 'Here, doggy; here, doggy.' We're not going to find him sitting under a tree somewhere, trying to remember where he lives."

Twee pressed the doorbell, which blasted like a maximum-security prison alarm. We both jumped.

"God!" I said. "Maybe her dog left home to get away from that terrible bell."

Twee elbowed me. "Shhh! Maybe she's hard of hearing."

The front door pulled open, and Ginger looked out at us, beaming. She wore jeans, and her gray hair was pulled up in a soft bun. "Good morning, girls! You made good time on your bikes, didn't you?"

"YES, we DID! You GAVE us GREAT DIREC-TIONS," Twee shouted.

Ginger looked startled. "I'm glad, honey. Now why are you shouting?"

Twee reddened. "Sorry. I thought maybe, wull, maybe you—"

I broke in. "Your buzzer is very loud. We thought maybe you were a little hard of hearing. Some older people are," I added. "You might wear your hearing aids in public, but then maybe not wear them at home."

Ginger laughed, which triggered a short coughing spell. I turned my head away while she finished, remembering the cough Nana had for years. She kept saying it was "just a tickle" when Mom would insist she go to a doctor.

"Oh, my!" she said, trying to clear her throat. "No, my hearing is just fine. I had a special doorbell installed so I could hear it from my darkroom." She pointed over her shoulder, explaining, "I'm a photographer, and I develop my own film here at home.

"Please come in!" she said, waving us inside. "I'll just dash into the kitchen and get our refreshments. Now," she said, motioning to the living room, "make yourselves right at home."

That was all the invitation Twee needed. She crossed the room, making her way toward the fireplace and the collection of photographs on the mantel. She was insanely curious about people and their families.

I stood still and quiet, letting the house settle around me a moment. Houses, just like people, had a kind of personality all their own. Ginger's house felt comfortable, like a favorite old sweatshirt that had been washed to softness perfection. I lifted my nose slightly and took in the aroma of something warm and melty—like chocolate. Hopefully, it was part of the refreshments Ginger mentioned.

I passed a giant vase of roses on her dining-room table. I wondered if she had grown them all. I picked up one of the fallen petals from the table and smelled it. Homegrown, for sure. Store-bought roses never smelled that good.

I'd read all of Nana's old Nancy Drew books at least twice, and my favorite ones three times. If Twee and I were going to find this dog, we needed to start collecting clues, just like Nancy and her pals did. Details were key.

I ran a hand over the cushions on her couch and then leaned over and took a deep whiff. Strange, no dog smell. And no dog hair.

Well, maybe Mr. McWhat's-His-Face was a well-behaved dog that didn't sit on the furniture.

"Macy!" Twee whispered, in that special whisper of hers that could wake the dead. "Come look! She's got a picture of some guy up here . . . *and Chuck!*"

"What?" I turned and hurried over to the fireplace. *"Him?* Here?"

I stared up at the photograph in a shiny silver frame. Sure enough, Chuck and some guy were leaning against a railing, with an ocean sunset behind them. They were grinning at each other as if they'd just heard the world's best joke.

The kitchen door swung wide with a whoosh, followed by Ginger carrying a large tray. "Now listen, you two. If you don't care for German chocolate cupcakes, just say the word. I've got a box of lemon cookies in the pantry, too. So, don't be shy." She set the tray down on a big coffee table.

My knees grew weak. German chocolate was my favorite dessert in the world. How did Ginger know that? Had Twee told her? It was the birthday cake I picked every single year. Nana always made my cake, right up until she was too sick to do it. Mom keeps encouraging me to try something new and different, but I never do. When I love something, I stick with it. Wish I could say the same for my mom. She thinks we should welcome change, as if it were a natural and regular part of life. But change isn't "natural." And right at that moment, too much change was exactly what was wrong with my life.

"There, I think that's everything!" Ginger surveyed

the table and began pouring milk into glasses. Her hand was a little shaky. "The cupcakes are optional, but the milk is not. Young ladies like you two need your calcium."

Twee licked a ring around the top of her cupcake and sighed, the picture of contentment.

"Uh, this is supernice of you, but we can't stay too long," I said. Ginger seemed like she was a pretty cool lady, but I didn't have a whole lot of time. I told Twee I'd give it my best shot until Wednesday, but that was it. The rest of the week was mine.

I wouldn't *mind* finding her dog, of course. And I'd be lying if I didn't admit I'd been daydreaming about everything I could do with my split of the reward.

"I have some questions I need to ask you about Mr. McDuffy," I started in.

Twee kicked me sharply in the shin and mouthed, "McDougall."

"Er, I mean, McDougall— Sorry," I said, flustered.

"That's okay, honey. It's a funny name to remember."

"Well," I continued, getting to business, "exactly how long has he been gone?"

Ginger wiped her forehead with the back of her hand. "Well, let's see—I was in the darkroom developing prints, and I usually do that on Mondays."

"Was it last Monday?" Twee asked.

"No, not last Monday," she said, her voice fading. She paused a moment and then took her glasses off and wiped them on her shirt. "Maybe the Monday before? He's been gone awhile now."

I took a big, unladylike bite into my cupcake. My taste buds nearly exploded with happiness. I took a long swig of milk, so I could speak again. It was all I could do then not to spit it all into my lap. The milk was sour. I managed to get it all down, just barely. I tried to give Twee a warning glance, but she was headfirst in her cupcake and oblivious.

I took another bite of mine to get the curdled taste out of my mouth. "Has he been gone more than a month?" I asked finally.

She nodded, her voice soft. "By now I suppose it must be."

"And where was he when you last saw him?"

"He was lying—" she started, and then cut herself off. She shut her eyes a moment, and I could see the tiny blue network of veins on her eyelids.

It made her look so fragile, like Jack when he was sleeping. Her chin twitched for a split second.

My throat grew thick. I cleared it hard. I didn't have any space left inside me for Ginger's sadness. I was filled to the brim with my own.

Twee reached over and touched Ginger's sleeve. Ginger patted Twee's hand. I looked down at the enormous oars that were my hands and tucked them under my legs.

"He was sleeping in his bed, peaceful and sweet, last time I saw him." She twisted a heavy, silver band on her finger and took a long breath. "Then I went to work in my darkroom for a while. When I came out for lunch, he was gone." She picked an imaginary crumb from her lap. "I'm afraid that's all I can tell you about his disappearance. It was a nice day, so the back door was open. He could have gotten out through the gate if he'd a mind to. There's a neighbor cat that sits on the top of the fence and taunts him. It made him crazy. He'd bark till he was hoarse. Usually, I'd hear him and chase the cat away, but as I said, I was in the darkroom." Ginger leaned over and moved things around on the coffee table, looking to distract herself.

"Do you take pictures for fun, or is it, like, your job?" Twee asked, a piece of coconut hanging from her lip like a comma. I reached over and removed it.

"I was a photographer for the military for thirty years. I first started in Vietnam and later in the Persian Gulf." She seemed relieved to talk about something else. "Then when I retired I started freelancing. So, it's fun *and* it's work, I suppose."

Twee's eyes bulged. "You were in Vietnam?"

Oh, no. I did not want Twee going off on a tell-me-of-my-homeland binge right now.

"Yes, for quite some time, actually. Are you Vietnamese, Twee?"

Twee nodded dumbly, too excited to speak.

"I've been curious since you told me your name. I knew a shopkeeper in Haiphong named Tui."

I jumped up and reached a hand out to Twee. "We need to get going, really. Thank you for the refreshments."

"Macy, hold on!" Twee said. "I didn't get a chance to drink my milk yet." Twee reached for her glass, and I had no choice but to grab it out of her hand. I didn't want her to drink it. She had a much more sensitive stomach than I did. I took three long gulps of it and then used all my powers of concentration not to spit it back out.

"Geez, Macy, what are you doing? You didn't even finish your own milk." She looked at me like I was out of my mind.

I wiped my mouth with the back of my hand. "Bikeridemademereallythirsty," I said, out of breath.

Twee shook her head. "Well, I guess so!"

"Oh, girls, there's plenty for both of you. Let me go get you some more—"

"No thanks, really!" I said.

"I'd love some," Twee insisted. "I'm thirsty from the bike ride too."

As Ginger walked across the room to the kitchen, I made a choking sign with my hand around my neck.

"What is *wrong* with you, Macy?" Twee whispered.

I grabbed the sleeve of my sweatshirt and tried to wipe out the inside of my mouth to get rid of the bad taste. "That milk expired sometime last year, I think!"

"Oooohh," she said. "Well, why didn't you just say something?"

"I dunno! I didn't want to make her feel bad. She went to so much trouble to make a nice snack for us."

Twee patted my knee. "You are such a softie."

Ginger came back into the room just then and seemed distracted. She put one hand on her hip. "Now, what was it I was going after? Lord, I hate when that happens."

I prayed a silent prayer of thanks to the dairy gods for saving us from more bad milk.

"Gosh, I do that all the time," Twee said. "We're fine, but we do need to get going."

"Ginger, do you mind if I look around a bit before I go?" I asked.

"Sometimes Macy gets special hunches," Twee explained. "It's kind of like being psychic, but instead of seeing things in the future, she sees things backward." She looked over at me. "That's how it works, right, Macy?"

"I'm sure Ginger isn't interested," I said.

"Actually, I am!" Ginger said.

I shrugged. "It's no big deal. I just notice things other people miss. Anyone can do it if they really pay attention. So . . . is it okay if I look around, Ginger?"

"Certainly, whatever you need," she said, tidying up the tray. "And I hope you're the ones who find him. I'd love to give you girls the reward money. That young man Twitch who came by last night was certainly pleasant, though. Said he'd heard from Chuck that he'd caused an accident, so he dropped by to apologize. Wasn't that nice of him?"

Twee and I exchanged wary glances. We both knew instantly who "Twitch" was. But Switch—*nice*?

Ginger continued. "He saw my flyers while he was here and said he'd scout around for Mr. McDougall while he was out 'making his rounds,' as he called it."

Twee blurted, unable to be still a moment longer. "If we find him, my half of the money is going toward a trip to Vietnam. I already have four hundred and thirty dollars saved so far."

Ginger put a hand on her shoulder. "You'll have to come back when you have more time to see my photos.

47

The countryside there is more beautiful than anyone imagines. If you have just a second, let me show you this amazing landscape I have hanging in my office."

Twee's mouth was open, and I half expected her to start drooling onto the floor. I nudged her. "Go ahead. I'm going to look around, and then I'll be out in the yard."

I rounded up the glasses of milk chunks and carried our plates toward the kitchen. I paused to study a large photograph of Mr. McDougall. He was lying on the couch, his head in a man's lap. It was the same man in the picture with Chuck. The guy had very white teeth and a nice smile. I was dying to know who he was and what he and Chuck were doing on Ginger's mantel. I had hoped Twee would ask, but she didn't. Twee is the queen of snoopy, embarrassing questions when you *don't* want her to be. But when you need her to be, she falls down on the job.

I sighed and made a mental note to ask Ginger when she'd had her furniture cleaned last. That would help us get a better idea of how long her dog had been gone.

I poured out all the milk and dumped our plates on the kitchen counter. As I turned to leave, two ceramic bowls on the floor in the corner caught my eye. Both were full to the brim—one with water, one with dry dog food.

I picked up a piece of dog food and rolled it between my fingers. It was still sort of crumbly, not hard, and smelled fresh. Fresh as the cupcake I'd just polished off. Strange. I walked over and opened her pantry door. And if I could whistle, I would have then—one of those long, amazed notes.

All six shelves of Ginger's tall pantry were packed with dog food, sacks and sacks of it. I moved to the overheard cupboards next to the pantry. Same exact thing. Nothing but dog food, dog biscuits, and dog treats.

I stood back and tried to sort this all out. Only one answer popped into my head.

Ginger must be stuck—like when you have a bad scratch on a CD and it just keeps playing the same thing over and over. *She must be buying dog food and leaving it out like Mr. McDougall isn't even gone,* I thought. *And she probably would keep doing it until someone stopped her.*

From the look of it, she'd been stuck for quite some time. My gut and my nose were telling me there hadn't been any Mr. McDougall around here for months.

Dear Mr. Jimenez,

The Second Thing About Me: my mom is a probation officer for kids, and my dad was an Airborne combat hero who fought in Iraq. Now he's working on a special project for the government, so he is going to miss parents' night. If my mom says anything bad about him, just ignore her. She probably won't in front of you, but sometimes she gets a very stern look on her face about him. Dad told me that hormones from having a baby make her very sensitive. Twee's mom, who is pregnant, has them too. (I am supposed to start getting hormones when I turn thirteen, but don't worry, I'll be in eighth grade then, and you won't be my teacher.)

Unless you have considered my request for you to flunk me back to sixth grade. Then I would be thirteen when I finally make it to your class. But I give you my word that when the hormones come, I will still be your best student ever.

Yours very sincerely,

Macy L. Hollinquest

PS I was sick last March for a whole week and missed learning about possessive pronoun's and contractions. Even though I studied Twees' note's, Im not sure I understood it. If you won't be covering that this year, that's' another good reason I should repeat sixth grade.

CHAPTER FOUR

Just the sight of the Greyhound bus station on Anacapa Street was enough to jangle my nerves. *C'mon, get a grip, girl. This is just a practice run.* I wiped my hands on the front of my shorts and then checked my watch. The southbound would be in any minute now.

Dad once confessed to me that he'd been super-scared the first time he had to jump out of a plane in the army. But earning his wings had been more important than anything, especially the fear. So the week before his first solo jump, he'd gone and talked to the jumpmaster. He'd told my dad that instead of focusing on the jump, he should just think about all the steps that came before that. The jumpmaster said if he did all those things right, the jump would take

* * * * *

care of itself. Dad said he'd practiced getting his gear straight, packing his chute, breathing, and counting. His first jump went great, and he'd learned to love it. He'd done a ton more jumps after that because to him it was easy.

That was what all I had to do today. Just go through all the steps and try to breathe. The rest would take care of itself.

Bus number 17 downshifted with a big whine as it turned wide into the station. It was smoky and hot, like hell on big, wide tires. The exhaust filled my mouth with tar, and a cold sweat wet my armpits.

It was the same deal every time. Just like the first day of kindergarten, when I'd waited on the curb in my new Dora the Explorer sneakers. I couldn't wait to start school like the big kids on my block. But Dad had been home on leave for just a few short days that time. I was torn right in two over wanting to be with him every second, but dying to go. I'd been waiting my whole life for it!

I tried to wake him up before I left, even though Mom said not to. I wanted to make him promise not to do anything fun until I got home.

But he was supertired that morning, and I couldn't even get him to open his eyes. I still remember taking his car keys out of his pants pockets and hiding them in my room. I'd seen Mom do that too, when she wanted him to know she loved him a lot and didn't want him to go away.

At the bus stop that day, Mom was quiet and held my hand too tight as we waited. When the big yellow bus finally came, it blew hot smoke right into my face. The oily smell made my head feel kind of dizzy. The bus seemed very big and scary up close. And it was so loud. I tried not to look nervous in front of all the other kids as I tiptoed on to the bus and took a seat as close as I could to the bus driver.

She looked big and scary up close, too. Maybe she didn't even like kindergartners! I pressed my face against the window, making sure my mom was still on the sidewalk. She was waving and blowing kisses at me. And she was even crying a tiny bit.

The bus lurched away from the sidewalk. After one block my breakfast had started to grow inside my stomach. I felt fuzzy and swimmy—like the time Aunt Liv let me eat a chili dog and fries and then drink a whole bottle of root beer by myself. I had a bad feeling about what might happen next.

Then it happened. I bent over in my seat and threw up all over my new sneakers. And hoped none of the other kids would notice. But then I threw up on the back of the bus driver's head. That got their attention right away. My name at school for a long time was Barferella.

All these years later, I still got icy sweats just being near a bus. It was so lame. I shivered beneath my hoodie.

The driver climbed out, squeezing a pair of giant hips through the narrow exit. He waited while the passengers got out. Everyone looked like they'd just woken up. They all had big hair dents in the back of their heads.

"Tweenty minute stop, everyone!" he shouted. "Let's hurry back now."

I stared at the bus door . . . and the unexpected opportunity. I could get over two hurdles today—being near the bus and actually *getting on* it. I'd be way ahead of the game for Wednesday's trip.

I moved closer, and my gut began to boil. I backed away and sat down on the bench outside the station. I pretended I was tying my shoes and trying to keep from losing it. I did some mental calculations. Exactly how long would it take me to ride my bike to Los Robles? If I could ride 10 miles per hour, and Los Robles was about 102 miles away—uh, let's see, it would be about next Thanksgiving when I arrived. Chuck might be carving the family turkey at our house by then. And maybe even staying to tuck Jack in and then trying for some kissy face with Mom. Forget it. I was out of options. It was the bus or nothing if I wanted to get to my dad.

I took a bracing breath and then bolted for the bus door. I took three steps in one leap. Then hunkered down in the darkness behind the driver's seat and wiped the sweat from my lip. Bright lights danced across my vision. That was not a good sign.

Relax! My stomach began to roll in giant waves. Uh-oh. I looked around frantically for a trash can.

Nothing—except for a knitting bag, and I couldn't hurl on someone's afghan. I peered down the aisle toward the bathroom, which at the moment looked impossibly far. But it was closer than the restroom inside the bus station. My mouth filled with something very bad like battery acid. Hunched, I ran through the bus, down a nightmare's long dark tunnel, row after row after row of seats. Finally, I yanked open the narrow door and dove headfirst for the tiny steel toilet.

I waited for the torrent, an instant replay of everything I'd eaten in the last twenty-four hours. . . .

Waited.

Then waited some more.

For anything, really.

I heaved and hoed, but I was shooting nothing but

blanks. I gagged until I was nearly hoarse and then gave up. I sat back on my haunches, waiting for the world to stop spinning. I groped in the dark cubicle for a paper towel to wipe up the drool, the only thing I'd been able to come up with.

The door opened behind me. "Here, kid," a voice said, and a hand stuffed a paper towel into my hand. Mortified, I turned. *Switch* grinned down at me. "You've got some pipes there. You sounded like a rhino trying to chuck up a wild boar or something."

My face burned as I glared at him. I turned on the tiny faucet and splashed myself with the miniature stream of water. It smelled like it came from a swamp.

"Hey, don't get bent. I was kidding. Here," he said, handing me a piece of gum already out of the wrapper. "This will help."

I hesitated just a moment and then crammed it into my mouth, grateful for the taste of anything else. "What are you doing in here?" I hoped snottiness would hide my humiliation.

"Might ask you the same."

I shrugged a shoulder and tried to get my vision back in line.

He cocked his head and studied me. "I see you around the coffee shop, right? You hang out with that chick, Tweetie?"

"Twee," I said, with a look meant to maim. "And you almost got her killed yesterday. Not to mention knocking me on my keester!"

He passed me one of his famous slow and easy smiles. "Sorry about that."

"And you made this poor old lady crash her bike into Nana's window, a window that had managed to survive nearly thirty-seven years—until *you* wrecked it."

He opened his mouth, but I cut him off, lightning-quick. "Even worse, you rode off and left. That's hit and run, you know. It's against the law."

His brows crossed. "I made sure nobody was hurt before I took off. You just didn't see me."

"A decent person would have stayed and apologized!"

"I couldn't," he said. "I thought the cops might come, and I wasn't in the mood to see them." He ran his hands across his white-blond buzzed hair. "I did go over to that lady's house afterward. Made sure she was okay. Chuck told me where she lived. Heck, I even offered to help her find her lost dog."

I nodded suspiciously. "Yeah, she told me. She thought you were Mr. Manners in the flesh."

Switch looked past me out the window of the bus. "Here comes Big Boy." He backed up, snatched a paper sack and his skateboard off a seat, and hurried down the aisle. "Come on, kid. Unless you got a ticket, you better get off too."

I rushed out behind him, and we both vaulted into the street, not slowing down until we turned the corner. We skidded to a stop in front of a row of newspaper racks. I sucked in my breath, still feeling a bit green. Switch dug into his pocket and fed a quarter into the *Daily Post* machine. He lifted a dozen papers out in one swoop.

"What are you doing? You can't take them all," I said, indignant. "They're a quarter apiece, not a quarter a pile."

He shrugged.

"You gonna go sell them? That's classy," I said.

"I'm not gonna sell them."

"Oh, right, you're going to read them all yourself!"

He shifted the papers over to his bony hip. "They're not for me. There's a nursing home over in my old neighborhood. I take them there."

"You're stealing . . . for old people?"

"I'm not stealing; I'm delivering. I hand out some papers and wish a few old geezers a good morning. They like having a fresh paper of their own. Not the day-old ones that the staff leave around."

"It's still not right," I said, thawing slightly.

"You should just ask the *Post*. Maybe they'd donate the papers, and then you wouldn't have to raid their machines."

"You call it raiding; I call it goodwill."

"Let me see if I get this: you've got a big soft spot for old people, but you hate veterans?"

"What are you talking about?" he asked.

"I suppose you think you got away with it, but I *saw* you throwing stuff at the veterans' float at the parade a couple years back."

Switch's expression didn't change, but a muscle in his jaw flickered. He spun the wheels of his board with his hand.

"Remember? You were up on the roof of my nana's coffee shop. I saw you from down below."

"I remember."

"My *dad* was on that float! You nailed him with a water balloon!"

"Sorry 'bout that. I wasn't trying to hit *him*. I was—" He shifted the papers on to his other hip. "You know what? Just forget it."

I could feel the spit gathering at the side of my mouth, like it does when I'm really mad. I swiped at it.

"You're kind of sweet when you're mad," he said. He reached over and tucked a piece of hair behind my ear. "I respect that."

I untucked the hair out from behind my ear and changed the subject. "So you really are going to help Ginger?"

"Who's Ginger?"

"The woman who you could have killed yesterday?" I rolled my eyes. "The one you went and apologized to?"

"Oh, her, right. Hey! Why don't we look for her dog together?"

"No way. Twee and I are going to find him, and we aren't splitting the reward with anyone."

"Fine by me. I don't want reward money. I just wanted to help her out. And since I already have a lead on the pooch," he said, backing down the street, "I thought maybe you might be interested."

"Well, wait a dang sec," I yelled.

"You chicks have at it. Good luck!" He slammed his board onto the sidewalk, jumped on, and sped away.

Leaving me wondering if I'd just been had. Or not.

Monday afternoon, I kicked my soccer ball up onto the porch. Then I fell into our old creaky porch swing, bone tired. I'd made the Kit Carson team, but just barely, I think. Coach Reeves was surprised, though, to see me show up. He'd been hoping I'd come to basketball tryouts instead. He lived in my neighborhood and watched me play for years in the cul-de-sac that had a hoop set up.

My dad was not a basketball person. He was pretty terrible at it. I could outdribble him and outshoot him by the time I was eight. He said basketball was an easy game for lazy athletes and that if I really wanted to develop skills, soccer was the only way to go. Soccer, he was great at, and he'd played all through school. He loved showing me all his moves. I was working at it. My feet were kind of all thumbs.

I peeled off my shoes and ripe, steamy socks. I slumped back in the swing and closed my eyes. I was glad tryouts were over. My stomach was so empty it felt like a dried-up old raisin. I closed my eyes and gave in to the sway of the swing.

I wished Dad were here so I could tell him that I'd made the team. He'd be really happy.

I remembered the last time I'd sat out here with him. Mom was mad at him about something, so he and I had escaped the house together. It was raining like crazy, and he took my hand to read my palm. He said a fortune-teller would probably charge me extra because my hand was so big. Kind of like how car washes charge extra for trucks and vans. We laughed about that. Then I teased him that he could get a half-price special at a manicurist, because his nails were so short—he had them bitten down nearly to the moons. Sometimes he peeled the sides down until they bled. It drove Mom crazy.

God, I wished he would just come home. Seemed like I'd spent my whole life waiting for him. Even after I was first born, it had taken him two days to get to the hospital to meet me. I'd once figured out that in my whole lifetime, I'd been away from him more than I'd ever been with him.

When Nana first got sick and the army let him out early to run the café, I thought we had him for good. But then Mom went and ruined it all. To her, whatever Dad did was wrong. When he'd have to stay late at the café, she'd get mad. When he had to go on business trips to buy supplies, she'd stomp around the house with her lips sewn up tight.

When she got pregnant with Jack, I was so glad. I figured it would change everything. Mom would finally be happy, and Dad would stay home forever. No such luck in my sorry life. Instead, it was like watching a long line of dominoes fall—

Nana's cancer starts to spread like a wildfire—*clack-clack-clack-clack-clack*—

Dad is so sad he can hardly work—*click-click*—

Mom gets even madder at him—*click-click-click*—

Mom talks everyone into selling Nana's shop—*clackety-clackety*—

Nana dies—*click-clack-click-clickclickclickclick clickclickclick*—

Dad disappears—*clackety-clackety-clackety-clackety—Chuck!*

Now I wait every single day for Dad to come home. Mom and I used to wait together, but it's changed. It feels like she stopped waiting.

"PeekaBOO!" Sticky, wet hands pawed at my eyelids. "Peek-a-me!"

"GENTLE, Jack!" I yelled, rolling over in the swing so he couldn't poke my eyes out. He climbed up behind me and tried to turn my head around, so he could continue a round of peekaboo, just about the dumbest baby game ever invented. Resisting was pointless, so I flopped over onto my back and pulled him up onto my stomach.

"Okay, okay, Jack, enough with the peekaboo!" I grabbed both his chubby little hands and pretended I was going to eat them, which always horrified and thrilled him. He threw his head back, screaming and laughing.

"It's time to play Hide the Baby! Yay! Yay!" I clapped his hands together.

He screamed, drool hanging from his chin. He

slid down off the swing and stood waiting, one small hand on my leg, his eyes big. He farted into his big diaper and then jumped, startled, his nerves already on edge.

"Reaaady?" I said. "Seeeett?"

He bounced up and down, chiming in "Gooo?"

"HIDE THE BABY, JACK!"

Squealing like a piglet, he pounded across the porch in his baby high-tops, ripping into the house. He'd always hide himself under his little bed or my mom's bed. Never my bed, though, not since I'd put up Cookie Monster. Jack was a whiz at the game. He could hide for a good ten minutes before he came hunting for me. Unless he fell asleep where he was hiding. That was always an unexpected bonus.

I loved him so much it nearly made me ache, but that didn't mean he didn't drive me nuts sometimes. It was hard being adored twenty-four hours a day. My dad was crazy about him too. Aunt Liv told me he broke down and cried when they first put Jack into his arms. Said that now he had everything he ever wanted in the world—first a daughter, and now a son. I knew it was really hard for him to be away from Jack. Babies change so fast, and Dad was missing so many of Jack's firsts.

The screen door opened back up, and Mom came

out. "Macy, I wish you wouldn't do that to him. If you don't want to play with him, just come get me."

"I am playing with him! He likes hiding."

"No, he loves playing with his big sister. Why don't you read to him or put him in the stroller and take him for a walk?"

"Tryouts went well, by the way. I made the team."

"Oh, Macy, that is so fantastic! I was just going to ask—"

I leveled her a look. "I'm sure you were. You're a very polite mother."

She drew in a breath, and I could tell I'd gotten to her.

"If Dad were home, he would have been at my soccer tryouts."

"Let's not do this right now, okay? You're tired and hungry. Come in and get something to eat. I'm up to my armpits in grocery sacks, and I've got a runaway that work is calling me about. But first, I need to get out for a run. I've missed the last three days."

"Can't you go later? I have stuff I need to do too!" I kind of made that part up, but I wasn't feeling very cooperative.

"I'm running with someone, so I can't reschedule."

"Who?" I asked, suspicious. She usually ran alone.

"I bumped into Chuck while I was out shopping.

He had a lot of questions about the supplier contracts we used. I didn't have time to talk, so I suggested if he wanted to go out for a run with me, I'd fill him in."

It took me a minute to digest this. First the phone calls, now running dates?

"Oh!" she said, looking out across the yard and then at her watch. "Here he comes already. I better go change." She waved at him as he slowed to a jog and then stopped in front of our house. He pulled the cap off the water bottle he carried and took a swig. "Hey, there!" she called out to him. "Give me five minutes. I'll be right down."

He nodded and wiped his forehead with the inside of his elbow. He gave me a small wave and then stretched his hairy calves against our tree.

I stared at him, still not believing he had the nerve to come onto our private property like this and, even worse, planned to go on a run with my mother. I thundered down the walkway toward him. When I reached him, I stood glaring at him while the thousand things I wanted to say fought to get out first.

"Hey, Macy. How'd tryouts go?"

"Wha*aat*?" I asked, exasperated that he'd been the first to speak and that he knew anything about my life.

"I heard you were trying out for soccer—"

"Who told you that?"

He folded his leg behind him and pressed his toe into his backside, stretching his quads. "Uh, I'm not sure. I overhear a lot at the shop."

More glowering from me. "You sure have a *lot* of questions about running a coffee shop. Did it ever occur to you that if you still have this many questions after doing it for over a year, that maybe you're not cut out for it?" There, I'd finally gotten one good shot out there.

He didn't look like he'd been hit at all. He just gave me a friendly smile and said, "Well, I sure don't know as much as your nana did, and I don't know what I would have done if I didn't have your mom to help me."

I felt like a big bull snorting and pawing in the dirt, and *he* just wouldn't wave the red cape like he was supposed to. It was maddening.

"Caffeine Nana's is a dumb name. You should have left it just plain old Nana's."

He shrugged and nodded. "You may be right. It seemed like a good idea at the time."

Mom came down the walkway just then in her extremely skimpy running shorts and top. It was what she always wore, but still, it griped me. She should have worn something that covered up her curvy parts.

"Your mom tells me it's almost your birthday," Chuck said, turning his glance back to me. "Any fun plans?"

"Ab-so-lute-ly *none!*"

I turned and gave Mom a look that would spoil meat. She had Jack in her arms, and she handed him off to me. I tried to shield him from Chuck's view, but Jack squirmed around so he wouldn't miss anything. The little Benedict Arnold put up his pudgy hand for a high-five. Chuck gently slapped it. Jack laughed and drooled and then put his hand up for more. I twirled him around at that.

I thundered back up the walkway toward the house. Apparently, I lived in a whole house full of traitors.

CHAPTER FIVE

I grabbed Twee's shirt and yanked her toward me, one half second before she plowed right into a parking sign. She would have been seeing stars for days. But Twee was used to me steering her and kept right on talking, not missing a beat.

"Of course, most of the reward money would go toward my trip, but I'm going to take forty dollars to buy those green suede boots at Girls West." She twirled, as if she imagined how they'd look on her.

I cut her off at the pass. "You keep forgetting the minor detail that first we actually have to find Mr. McMuffin."

"McDougall, Macy! It's Mr. McDougall! Could you at least get his name right?"

"McWhatever. And you need to get your mind off

* * * * *

of the reward money and pay some attention to this dog hunt. You know, maybe we should let Switch in on this with us. He did say he had a lead."

"If he does have a good lead, what does he need us for? He doesn't exactly strike me as the sharing type."

We traipsed across the grass of Jet Park, named for the old jet that sat in the middle of it. Years ago the city had gutted the plane and cleaned it up. It had been my first jungle gym. I knew every curve and hollow of that plane.

We settled down in our favorite spot in the shade of the jet's wing. I rolled over onto my stomach and unwrapped a peanut butter sandwich on big slices of sourdough bread. Twee took the lid off a container of rice. She'd started eating Vietnamese food almost exclusively, like if she ate enough of it, her birth parents might just show up. Not that she wanted to leave her family here in Constant, but probably like other kids who were adopted, a part of her was always thinking about her other life. The one that she might have lived.

I opened my sandwich and ripped open a bag of M&Ms. I planted colorful rows into the gooey deliciousness of peanut butter. I slapped the top back on and sank my teeth into it. It was a good sixty seconds before I could speak again. I took a long swig from a canteen my dad brought me from his first trip to Baghdad. I tried to bring up the subject of Switch again. "Well," I said, clearing my throat, "you know, if he does have a clue, it could be worth some money. Maybe we should just offer him a cut, maybe fifty bucks, for his info, *if* we find the dog."

She looked at me, shaking her head. "No way. If he does know something, which I completely don't believe, he learned it yesterday when he was cruising Ginger's neighborhood. Heck, we can do that." She grabbed my sandwich and took a big bite, moaning when she hit my chocolate crop.

I took a whiff of something she'd brought in her jar and then moved it away from me fast. It smelled like someone had died in that jar.

Twee wiped her mouth with the back of her hand. "So, what do you think he was doing on the bus, Macy?"

I snatched my sandwich back. "I dunno." A quick rush of guilt flooded me. I'd told Twee I was at the bus station buying her ticket when I'd run into Switch.

She waved a carrot stick at me. "You know, I heard Cynthia Ramos tell my sister that they can't hardly keep Switch in foster homes. He just up and leaves when he feels like it."

"So?"

She stared hard at me. "So, nothing. Just thought

you might be interested since you can hardly stop talking about him."

"What's that supposed to mean? I've said two sentences about him all day." I felt my face color.

"Oh, c'mon. It's been nothing but 'Switch, Switch, Switch' around here since Saturday. First you won't stop talking about him because he beans you on his board. Then you're all fired up because Ginger thinks he's a nice boy. He's Robin Hood Junior stealing newspapers for the poor. And now, of course, he holds the case-cracking clue that would lead us right to Mr. McDougall." She paused for a moment and looked off into space. "But no, other than that, you haven't really mentioned him much."

I balled up my trash and got to my feet. "Are you done? Let's go. We're burning daylight here."

The clatter of skateboard wheels nearby made me jump. My head whipped in their direction. But it was just some little kid wearing a helmet. Not a big kid with long feet and brush-cut hair. I was disappointed, and I didn't even know why.

Twee snapped a bite of her carrot stick and glowered at me. "I rest my case."

An hour later I parked myself on the back fender of an old pickup across the street from Ginger's house.

Twee and I had split up so we could cover more territory in the neighborhood. I'd probably knocked on twenty doors, enough to send my mother to an early grave.

I hadn't run into any real psychos, but the man in the green house on the corner did ask me if I knew Jesus. Then he threw his head back, opened his mouth wide into a giant O, and belted out, "He's my Loorrrrdd, He's my Guiiide, He's my Ladderrr to the Skiies!"

I split before verse two, no disrespect intended to the Big Ladder.

The old lady in the tiny house with the sign "Beware of Killer Cats" insisted on giving me a dollar, even though I kept telling her I wasn't selling anything. I put the dollar back in her mailbox when she closed her door.

The only worthwhile piece of information I'd discovered was that those who actually knew Mr. McDougall hadn't seen him for months. "Curiouser and curiouser," I mumbled. Of course, he was an old dog, so maybe he hadn't gone out much in the last year. Or maybe my hunch was right, and he hadn't been around in a long time.

Twee hurried down the sidewalk toward me, pulling a young kid by the arm of his shirt. He was probably eight or nine and looked like he'd made the acquaintance of way too many pizzas. Twee stood next to him, beaming, like she was showing a prize heifer at the county fair.

"Go on. Tell her what you told me," she said, bumping him with her elbow.

He looked at me over a juice Popsicle while sticky rivers of red ran down his pudgy arm. "Pay up," he said to me. He pointed his chin toward Twee. "She said you would."

"Do what?"

"Oh, yeah. You have to pay him, Macy. It was the only way he'd come down here. I already gave him a buck. Give him another, and he'll sing."

"Sing?" My best friend had apparently turned into a gangster since I'd last seen her. "And why am I paying for information that you already have?" I asked her.

"Because I promised you would. And because some of it's about Switch. I thought you should hear it from the kid yourself."

I dug deep into my jeans and pulled out a wad of rumpled cash. My piggy bank had suffered a serious hit this morning. I had taken out my trip money for Los Robles, plus some extra for investigation expenses. I pulled a George Washington away from the pack and held it out to him. He reached for it, but I held it away.

"Nope. First you talk. Then if I think what I hear is worth it, I'll pay."

The kid had his mouth planted on the end of the Popsicle, making gross sucking sounds. Like Jack used to do when he was nursing. I took the Popsicle out of his mouth and handed it over to Twee.

"Hey! Give it back!" he cried, all little boy now.

"I will just as soon as we finish our deal. It's not polite to eat, and really not polite to slurp while you're doing business. Now, do you want the money or not?"

He wiped his mouth on the soft inside of his arm. He sighed. "Okay, s'like I already told her," he said, pointing his chin at Twee. "Mr. McDougall isn't lost. I keep trying to tell Ginger that, but she won't listen. Every time I try, she gives me a cookie and tells me to run on home."

"What do you mean he's not missing? Are you saying she's making this up?" I asked. I shot a look over at Twee and then back to the kid.

"Oh, he's missing all right. He's just not lost." He pulled his T-shirt down over his sizable boy boobs, which, for the record, were bigger than Twee's and mine combined. He leaned in toward me and whispered, "He was *kidnapped!*" He paused while Twee and I shot wild looks at each other. "And right before my eyes," he added.

"Kidnapped!" I repeated, incredulous.

"Yep, kid-napped." He rolled back on his heels, letting it sink in but dying to tell more. "Round 'bout last February, on a weekday. I was home, sick from school, lying on my couch, just looking out the window. I live right there, the one with the Christmas lights." He pointed. "I see this guy pull up in Ginger's driveway in some kind of delivery van. He comes out a few minutes later carrying something all covered up in a blanket. I thought maybe it was laundry, but then I saw a long tail hanging out."

Twee and I stared at each other, our eyes big.

He continued. "It was Mr. McDougall's tail! And the kidnapper was talking to him. I could see his mouth moving, like maybe he was telling him to shut up or something." He paused, his forehead clouded with the remembering.

"*Then* what?" I said, my impatience like a bulldozer pushing him on.

The kid shrugged. "Then the kidnapper guy laid him in the front seat of the truck and drove off."

Twee shook her head. "Did you call 911?"

"No way," he said. "I'm not allowed. Not unless I'm

on fire. That's what my dad says. I did tell my mom, though. She told me to stop spying on the neighbors."

"This is unbe*liev*able," I said. I stared over at Ginger's, trying to visualize it all. "Tell me more about the van. Did it have any writing on it?"

"Yeah, but I couldn't really read it. The writing was sort of loopy and fancy. I couldn't read the first word, so I gave up."

"Was there anything else on the van that you remember?" I pushed, but gentler now, not wanting to scare away any valuable clue.

He screwed his face up, thinking. "Nooo, nothing else. Except . . . ," he said, his face lighting up, "the wheels had custom mags, definitely not factory issue. Dual tones. Trailblazer tires. Urban squealers, they call 'em; steel belted, sixty-five-thousand-mile warranty, run you about hundred twenty-five bucks apiece."

"Thank you, Mr. Goodyear," Twee said. "How do you know all that?"

He shrugged. "I like cars."

"But can you remember anything useful," I pressed, "like what color the van was?"

"Hmmm . . . Well, some dark color, for sure. Maybe blue or green or brown. Oh! Oh!"

"What?" Twee and I screamed in harmony.

"Little lima beans!" he said, triumphant.

We looked at each other, puzzled, and then back at him. "Lima beans?" I asked.

"Yep, bunches of them—next to the writing."

Just then, a woman with lungs the size of Texas stuck her head outside the kid's front door and bellowed, "BUSSS*TTTER*! Get home right now!"

"Gotta go. S'my mom," he added, putting his palm up for the money.

Twee handed him his drippy Popsicle, but I held on to George. "One more thing. Did you tell all this to a kid on a skateboard a couple of days ago?"

He nodded. "Uh-huh. He gave me nearly a pocket full of quarters, and a candy bar. Said if I remembered anything else, or if anybody came sniffing around on the case, he wanted to know what and who. Said to leave him a note."

"Leave him a note where?" I asked.

"On the left wing of the plane at Jet Park. Under one of the flaps. He called it his 'mailbox.' Said his initials were on it. Cool, huh? I'm gonna get me a secret mailbox, too, and then—"

Twee interrupted. "Did you tell him everything you told us?"

"Not the part about the brown lima beans. 'Cos I just now remembered that." He looked anxiously toward his house. "Look, I gotta go. Just give me my money like you said, okay?"

I handed him one buck and then pulled out another to go with it. He licked his lips.

"Okay, Buster. But keep the lima beans just between us. You got that?" I said.

He raised two juice-stained fingers in a poor imitation of a Boy Scout pledge. "Okey-dokey, Smokey."

He turned to run, and I reached for the neck of his shirt gently, reeling him back in. "You remember anything else, Buster, you leave me a note. Not the kid on the skateboard, me. You got that? I want you to try real, real hard to remember what the writing said on the van. I'll give you ten dollars for that."

"Ten bucks!" Twee elbowed her way in between Buster and me. "No way!" She looked at me, stunned, like I'd just promised the kid he could be our date for our junior prom.

I shushed her with a look that silenced her.

"You can leave me a note over at Caffeine Nana's, Buster. You know where that is over on Alameda?"

He nodded, solemn, ever the good double agent.

"Give it to Chuck, the owner. Tell him the note is for Macy and that I promised you a free double-chocolate mocha. He's good for it."

Buster ran his tongue over his lower lip. "With alotta whipped cream?"

"The works. Now, get out of here before your mom dies of old age waiting for you."

Buster hurried toward his house, hooting as he mounted the porch stairs, his life suddenly more exciting than he could bear.

I blew out a big gust and wiped the sweat off my forehead. This latest development changed everything! Twee and I traded a long, serious look, a silent conversation about our next move. Twin-speak had nothing on the two of us.

She bobbed her head in agreement. "Cops."

"Yep, let's try Divine—" I said.

"Doughnuts," she finished. "On our way to—"

I nodded. "The library."

Dear Mr. Jimenez,

The Third Thing About Me: I'm a very curious kid, so I just went by Kit Carson Middle School and looked in the window where I will have my homeroom with you. Your name was on the door. Someone forgot to lock your room, which I accidentally discovered when I turned the knob. I went and sat in the second row, fourth seat, which is where I sat in sixth grade at my old school. There is nothing but buildings outside your window. You should ask for a classroom with a better view. A kid could go crazy in there without any trees to look at.

I will let you know when my dad finally comes home, because you should invite him to come to our class as a guest speaker. Like I said before, he is an Airborne combat hero, which is about the bravest thing you can be. He is very inspiring, and funny, too. He can do push-ups with me standing on his back. Maybe you and he could have a push-up contest! If you're not already in shape, you better get to work on it.

Yours very sincerely,
Macy L. Hollinquest

CHAPTER SIX

Officer Marley had legs as long as a giraffe, and he kept trying to fold them under the table, but knees kept popping out everywhere. He took a giant bite into what looked like a small meat loaf but was actually a low-fat, no sugar, whole-wheat, apple-and-oat-bran muffin. What Nana called a "Why Bother? Muffin." Might as well just eat a bale of hay, she'd say.

He rolled his eyes upward, thinking, as he gnashed through his breakfast with large white teeth. I scooted my chair closer, trying to avoid the tangle of his legs.

"Maybe they weren't lima beans," I said. "Could be some other kind of beans." He dabbed at the corners of his mouth with a napkin. I stared at his hands. They were immense. His fingers had to be seven inches long. My longest was about four and a half. I

* * * * *

brought them out from their usual hiding place under my legs and laid them casually on the table. Next to his, mine looked downright dainty. I could marry a man with big, giant hands like Officer Marley.

"But then, I can't say I remember seeing any vans around here with any kind of beans detailed on them. And you don't remember anything else about the vehicle?" He took a long swig of coffee, never taking his eyes off me.

"No, that's all I remember, Officer. It was really stupid of me to leave my good bracelet on the van like that, but I didn't want to lose it." I leaned in confidentially. "I'm only supposed to wear it for dress up, but I guess I wanted to show it off." I lifted, and then dropped, my shoulders, faking embarrassment.

"Well, we all do things we shouldn't now and then. Just part of growing up." He grinned with a big piece of raisin blacking out his front tooth. Twee stepped hard on my foot under the table, alerting me to the presence of something gross. Yeah, like I could have missed it. I quickly revised my marriage plans to Officer Marley.

He pulled out a shiny pen from his front pocket and clicked its end with great ceremony. He sucked at the raisin on his tooth, making a vacuum with his upper lip and tongue.

Twee stepped on my shoe again. Gross plus.

"You say you looped the bracelet over the vehicle's antenna, miss?" he asked, his pen poised over his official pocket notebook.

"Right." I shuddered, as if the loss of this nonexistent bracelet was painful to consider. "We were playing, uh, well, a bunch of us were out playing—" My mind went blank, and I shot Twee a desperate look.

She bugged her eyes at me. She'd only agreed to sitting in on this conversation if she didn't have to tell any lies. She thought lying to cops was probably just one notch down from lying to priests or nuns.

"Football," I blurted. "Touch football."

"Right!" she said. "With this kid, Buster."

"And you know how that can go," I said. "With all that grabbing and shoving, I thought I'd better put my bracelet somewhere safe. This van was just sitting parked in the street, so I hung it over the antenna."

He stretched his legs out into the aisle, looked over at Twee. "Then next thing you know, you look up and the vehicle is splitsville, right?"

Twee gulped, looked over at me, back to him, and then nodded. I could see the sweat on her forehead. Mostly, it was supergreat having such an honest best friend, but now and then it would be helpful to have one willing to drop a whopper, even to a cop.

I steered us back to the beans. "So, we figure the bracelet probably is still hanging on the antenna. All we gotta do is find the van and get it back. That's where we hoped you might be able to help. It's a pretty small town, and you spend a lot of time in traffic, don't you?"

"I sure do, miss, and there's not much that gets by me. But I don't recall a van with custom mags, and lima beans drawn on the side panel." He held up one amazingly long finger, cocked his head to one side, and appeared to be listening to the hum of his radio, which was stuck under a strap on his shoulder. He adjusted the volume. "Wanda, I'm ten-seven at Divine Doughnuts, over."

The radio blasted with static. Followed by a garbled message from Wanda, who sounded like she was broadcasting from the bottom of the ocean.

"Roger that. I'm ten-forty-nine toward home base. ETA sixteen hundred hours, over and out." Officer Marley slid out from under the table and stood up, adjusting his scary-looking cop equipment. He had all but a portable guillotine hanging off his belt.

"Gotta go. Big meeting back at the station. We're picking the design for our new league bowling shirt."

He held an imaginary ball up to his eyes, with his fingers splayed in position, drew his arm back in slow-mo, and then rolled a strike right through the front door. "Check back with me in a couple days, girls. I'll keep my eyes open and ask some of the guys. Bet we'll crack the bean-and-bracelet caper." He gave us a wink, hitched his pants, and was out the door.

"Think he bought your story?" Twee asked, picking up his leftover muffin and biting off the end.

"Twee!"

She opened her jaw for another bite. "What? I eat when I'm nervous. You know that!"

I swiped the muffin from her, horrified. "You can't eat the leftovers from someone you don't know!"

"I bit the part that he hadn't touched. Besides, he's a cop—not really a stranger or anything. In Vietnam, people aren't as wasteful with food."

"This is Constant, Colorado. Nice children don't eat off other people's plates."

"Excuse *me*, Miss Vanderbilt." She got up and swiped crumbs off her pants. "In Vietnam, nice children don't *lie* to cops."

As far as I was concerned, there was no better smell in the whole world than a library. Even better than a German chocolate cake right out of the oven, and that was saying something. I ran my hands over the polished wood of the old table in my favorite corner. Libraries were like churches for books. When Jack gets older, I was going to bring him here and show him all my favorites. I tried to bring him a few months back, but he had just learned how to make kitty noises, and wouldn't stop mewing. The librarian kept shushing him with a stern look, and I didn't want him to grow up hating librarians or anything. They were really cool. Once you got to know them.

Twee was buried somewhere on the second floor in the travel section, planning her trip to Vietnam. I wanted to use the computer here to check car detailers that paint business signs. But I also wanted to check out if there were any local bean companies. My mom was too nosy for me to risk doing any of this at home. Not that she would care if I was researching a potential dognapper. But I didn't need her in any of my business right now.

I needed some quiet time to think, too. I felt like I was at the carnival riding the Scrambler without any safety bar. It was already Tuesday, and I was just hours away from my trip to Los Robles. It wasn't as if I would be able to find my dad the minute I got there.

And I still had to come up with a convincing cover for Twee about what I was doing tomorrow. I also needed a good story to tell my mom about what I was doing. And then I had to make sure Twee knew what that story was, so she could back me up with Mom.

I wrote Switch's name out on a small piece of recycled scratch paper that the library put by the computers. I drew a tiny skateboard under his name, spending more time on it than I had to waste. He was on my mind, though. I wanted to leave him a note in the jet to lead him off track. I didn't want him solving this before we did. Now that Twee had talked me into doing this with her, I was determined to find this dog and earn the reward money. It was the least I could do for Twee. Not every girl was as lucky as I was to have a world-class best friend.

But first things first. I had a family who was circling the drain. I needed to find Dad. I unzipped my backpack and pulled out the letter he sent me. I studied the return address. It read:

Montgomery Hollinquest
c/o DVA
1716 Sixth Avenue
Los Robles, Colorado 80904

After I had first gotten the letter, I'd asked Mom casual-like what "DVA" stood for, and she said she thought it was one of the scary ingredients in hot dogs. That couldn't be right. I doubted that the Department of Defense had hired my dad to work on hot dogs.

I had waited a couple of days and asked her what "c/o" meant, and Mom said it means that the address is not someone's personal address, but where they get their mail. Which meant he may or may not be there if I went. But if I went in person, at least there was a chance that he'd be there. But if he wasn't, I could at least nose around, and maybe I'd find out where he was.

In my life as a kid, I have discovered that grown-ups will never tell you anything over the phone. Once they hear your kid voice, forget it. But I've also discovered that in person, grown-ups will do just about anything for a kid. It's funny how that works. So, I had to go in person. There was no other way to get the job done. But I had a feeling this was going to kinda be like trying to find a needle in the world's most humongous haystack.

I googled "DVA" and ran my eyes down and up the long list that popped into view, my lower lip pinned by my teeth—Delaware Volleyball Academy, DaVita Healthcare, Department of Veterans Affairs. . . .

Veterans— Bingo! That had to be it! It made perfect sense that he would work for the Department of Veterans Affairs on a special project. Next, I did a search on "Veterans Affairs in Los Robles."

"1716 Sixth Avenue"—perfect match! I had just mowed down my haystack big-time. If I hadn't been in the library, I might have done a few backflips.

I leaned back in my chair and drew a big breath. I checked my watch. I didn't have much time left. I had to get my alibis worked out. Twee hadn't asked me yet what I was doing tomorrow, but I knew she was just biding her time. It was her way. Since I hadn't immediately volunteered why I couldn't babysit Jack tomorrow, she was circling around it to figure out how she would get it out of me.

I had way too many meatballs on my plate, as Nana would say. I was already starting to sweat tomorrow's bus ride. My stomach would be in shreds before daylight. I blew the air out of my lungs. I needed to do a mental dress rehearsal, like Dad talked about.

I scooted down in my chair a bit and shut my eyes. I tried to let my neck and shoulders go soft. I set the scene.

I watch myself getting off the bus in Los Robles after a smooth ride. I wave good-bye to the cute high school boy I'd been talking to during the trip. I march down Sixth Avenue, my backpack heavy with the box of homemade macaroons I'm bringing Dad—his favorite.

After two blocks an enormous sign welcomes me to the Department of Veterans Affairs. I pull open the heavy glass doors and then head for the information desk. A friendly security guard listens to my story, picks up the phone, and smiles at me. He explains that while it's highly irregular, he's been authorized to take me up to the eighth floor. He clears his throat and leans close to me. Whispers that whatever I see up there, I mustn't tell anyone. Ever.

The elevator trip lasts a long time, and I wonder if we're not going much higher than the eighth floor. Probably a secret headquarters! The doors finally open, and we step out. It's dim and quiet. The only light comes from a large sign overhead that reads "DVA, Special Projects."

I spy a water fountain down the hallway, and a soldier in combat fatigues is bent over it. I look up at the guard, my throat parched all of a sudden. He nods, understanding, and I hurry down the hall. The soldier straightens up, wiping his mouth with his hand, takes a look a me—

"Macy?"

My heart leaps. "Dad?"

The soldier hurries toward me and then wraps me in his big arms.

"Dad!" *I hug him back hard, shaking.* "I'm so glad I found you—"

He holds me away from him a second and smiles. But now, it's not Dad—

"CHUCK!" *I shout, horrified, breaking away.* "What are you doing here?"

I back away and spin toward the elevator, but now it's gone. Instead, Nana's coffee shop is there—but the front window is all boarded up and across it someone has painted "Caffeine Canine Heaven."

"What have you done?" *I yell at Chuck, whipping back toward him. But he's not there anymore. Ginger is there instead. She looks at me with sad eyes, shaking her head.*

"He's gone, Macy," *she says.*

"Who's gone?" *I shout at her, because I don't know if she means Chuck or Dad or maybe Mr.—*

"Macy! What'ya doing? Sleeping?" Twee gives me a soft karate chop between the shoulder blades.

I sit up abruptly and blink. I can taste the early stages of sleep mouth. "Wasn't sleeping, just thinking." I reach over and click out of the DVA page.

"Did you find anything?" she asks.

"Uh, no not yet."

"Hey, guess what? I forgot to tell you. I called Ginger and asked her when I could come over and see her slides. She invited me for Saturday night and said to come to dinner, too. She's going to cook Vietnamese, and she said she'd teach me a couple of her best dishes. We're going to have nuoc mam with rice and vegetables."

"What is it?" I said, almost afraid to ask.

"I just looked it up," Twee said, who seemed quite pleased with herself. "It's fermented fish sauce. Want to come? She invited you, too."

"Thanks, but I had fermented fish once in the school cafeteria, and it was enough to last me a lifetime." I checked my watch. "Whoops, we gotta go, Twee. I'm supposed to be at Aunt Liv's in an hour."

Twee smiled. "How is Cat Woman?"

I gave Twee a look. "Don't call her that. Besides, what about your cousin Ainsley with the green-and-purple dreads? Your family beats mine hands down in weirdness."

Twee giggled. "My mom just told me that Ainsley is grounded for a month. She went and had her eyebrows tattooed on. She was gone for hours, and by the time she got back, her eyebrows were puffed up like two raccoon tails. Ainsley blew her probation curfew big-time, but my aunt doesn't want your mom to know about it. I think my aunt is more scared of your mom than my cousin is."

I stood up, slinging my backpack over one shoulder. "I won't tell. My lips are locked. C'mon. We better go. And don't forget about tomorrow. You've got Jack duty, bright and early."

Twee shot me a look. "I know. I'll be there!" She zipped up her sweatshirt with great concentration. "Any chance of you ever planning to tell me about your date with Switch tomorrow?"

I dropped my jaw ready to protest—then stopped. Voilà! My alibi. Even though I was older than Twee, she was the one who was interested in boys. She just assumed I was too. I liked boys okay, but I liked them best on the basketball court. I loved kicking soccer balls against their shins, too.

I dragged up my most pitiful, guilty look. "O-kay, okay, I'm sorry! I should have told you."

She crossed her arms. "Where you going to meet him?"

"Jet Park," I lied.

"What time?"

I put my arm through the other strap of my backpack with extreme care, like it held a couple sticks of dynamite, while my mind raced ahead sorting the details. "I'm supposed to meet him around seven. I'm gonna do his newspaper delivery with him. You know, to the old folks."

"Uh-huh. You're going to go with him while he steals papers. Very nice. What's next on the crime spree?"

"Cut it out, Twee. It's not the bad kind of stealing."

"It's still wrong, Macy," she said, blowing her bangs out of her eyes with a sharp upward gust. "And you know it."

"Yeah? Well, what about that time we got someone else's order at Galaxy Burger? Remember? You sure snarfed up those fries that weren't even ours."

"We were, like, eight years old. And that's different. But never mind. What time are you going to be home? And what are you going to tell your mother?"

"Twee, you've gotta help me here," I pleaded. "I'm going to be gone all day. We're going to Raging Falls with some other kids." I was on a roll with the lying thing now. "Some kid's dad is driving us. So, I can't say I have to come home early. I don't want to sound like a total baby. What am I going to tell my mom?"

"That you'll see her in juvenile court?"

"Twee! Come on. Help me out. I promise if you cover for me, I'll devote every second of the rest of the week—heck, the rest of my life—to finding Mr. McDuffy."

"McDOUGALL!" she yelled.

I shoved her toward the library exit. "Shhh! Okay, relax—Mr. McDougall. Doesn't matter what I call him. What matters is we find him."

"You cross your heart that you'll help me? And you won't fall so madly in love with Switch tomorrow that you'll give him our important clue? And you absolutely have to take the lip gloss I gave you? But don't let him kiss you on your first date!"

I made a giant cross over my heart and nodded, holding my breath.

"Well, all right," she said with an exasperated sigh. "But we still have to think of something to tell your mom."

I bit back a big smile of relief. Yes! Twee was on board.

She unlocked her bike from the rack, thinking out loud. "What's something your mom always wants you to do that you don't want to do?"

"Floss?"

"Yeah, well, we can't tell her you'll be gone all day flossing. Something else. Something that she'd have a hard time checking up on."

I strapped my pack on the back of my bike with a bungee cord, trying to smoosh the contents down. "Well, we just have to cover the day part while she's at work. Then we can tell her I'm going to be with you for dinner and stuff. She won't ever check about that." I pulled an empty soda can from my pack and crumpled it. I tossed it overhand in a high arc toward a large garbage container on the curb. "Three points!" I cheered as it landed dead center.

"I wish you'd recycle, Macy. That's such a waste."

Our heads swiveled toward each other at the exact moment. Our eyes met, and we locked gazes. We grinned.

"The Green Angels," we said in synch.

"Do you think she'd really buy it, Macy? You're so terrible about recycling."

"It's perfect! Those kids get up at the crack of dawn, and sometimes they're out all day. It's the last week of summer. I bet they've got something going every day: trail cleanup, litter, hazardous-waste disposal, making jewelry out of old batteries—you name it."

"You know," she said, looking thoughtful. "If we could get her to believe you're interested, it's the perfect cover for us too, for when we go to Los Robles together on Thursday. I've been wondering what we were going to tell our folks."

"Right, right!" I said, faking some enthusiasm. Trying to keep all the schedules straight in my mind was giving me brain lock.

Schedule A: what Twee thought I was doing.

Schedule B: what Mom was going to think I was doing.

Schedule C: what I was actually doing.

"We're still going on Thursday, aren't we?" I could hear the small flame of hope in her voice that I had changed my mind.

"Well, I'm going for sure," I said. "You don't have to go at all."

"You're not going off after your dad without me. Don't even think about it." She passed me a look that I could hardly meet.

Twee and I saw eye to eye on just about everything except my dad. Well, him, and Switch. I think it started back a couple of years ago. It was the summer that Nana was so sick. Dad had just gotten out of the army. He and I had been spending a lot of time together, and I think Twee might have been a little jealous. She got real bent at him one day when the three of us went hiking up in the foothills. Dad was in one of his really stellar moods—singing and playing fun car games with us. Twee was very quiet and kept hanging on to the door. My dad drives a little fast, maybe, but he's a real pro. He can drive jeeps, giant trucks and tanks—just about anything on wheels. You couldn't be any safer.

We hiked for hours—my dad is in excellent shape. Twee was having a hard time keeping up.

Afterward, we were really exhausted and hungry. Dad forgot to pack a lunch. We stopped at this little grocery store on the way home, and Twee was the only one with any money. Dad borrowed it from her and bought us sandwiches but didn't get any food for himself. He bought a couple of beers and a cigar. That really burned her up. I paid her back later, because my dad forgot, but she'd been sort of frosty about him after that.

Twee patted my arm as she buckled on her helmet. "I'm going to Los Robles with you, got it?" she said.

Knowing her as I did, I knew she was already plotting what she was going to do to talk me out of this trip on Thursday, even if it meant slashing the bus's tires and hog-tying the driver.

I nodded past the topic, quick as I could. "See you tomorrow at six forty-five, okay? I want to try to get out of the house before my mom wakes up."

She rolled her eyes. "If you get caught for this—"

I held up my hands. "I know! I know! You didn't know anything about it!"

"It will be a miracle if either of us actually makes it to the new school year next week. We'll probably both end up in jail," she muttered.

I watched as she pedaled off. Twee was the most loyal person in the world. Which meant lying to her made me feel like a complete louse. But I'd make it up to her. I was going to find that dog if it was the last thing I did this side of twelve.

CHAPTER SEVEN

Two hazel eyes stared at me unblinking from the top of Aunt Liv's headboard. Miss Doodle purred like a brand-new moped. But she's fooled me before, and I had the scars to prove it. I wasn't going to be duped again by the meanest cat that ever lived.

"Okay, nice and easy—" I whispered over my shoulder.

Aunt Liv stuffed a giant towel in my hand. "Here! Don't forget the gloves," she whispered back.

I stuffed my hands into her gardening gloves, like a doctor headed off to surgery. Miss Doodle yawned wide, but her eyes never left me.

I took a steadying breath. "We're going to have to distract her so I can throw the towel over her."

Aunt Liv grabbed a lipstick from the top of her

* * * * *

dresser. "Got it!" She plucked off the cap and moved to the other side of the bed. "Miss Doodle! Lookie, lookie here!"

Miss Doodle turned her head, eyes riveted on the end of the tube. She adored lipstick. If cats could drive, Miss Doodle would be a permanent fixture down at the MAC lipstick counter at the mall.

I scootched the towel up closer. Her head snapped back toward me. She hissed like a snake, her mouth all fangs.

"Yoo-hoo, Miss Doo-dle!" Aunt Liv sang. "Over here— Look! Mama's putting on lipstick!"

Miss Doodle turned back toward Aunt Liv, and her mouth dropped open slightly. She'd be drooling in a second and then be putty in my hands.

In one swift move I threw the towel over the top of her and then grabbed her well-padded neck. I dragged her toward me, limp as a newborn lamb. That was the nice thing about this weird cat. The minute you covered her, she was had. You could probably wear her on your head all day as a turban, and she'd sit up there like a perfect angel.

Aunt Liv held the kitty carrier door open wide, and I loaded my hostage into her temporary cell. Aunt Liv slammed the door and stood back. Miss Doodle puffed up like a wild jungle cat, growling and spitting in my direction. I gave her my best werewolf imitation, baring my teeth.

"Oh, thank the gods!" Aunt Liv said, collapsing on the bed. "That's done for another year. Thanks, Macy! If it wasn't for you, this poor cat would never get to the vet. I just don't have the heart for it. I feel like such a traitor as it is."

"You're just like Dad," I said. "He couldn't ask a fly to leave the room without worrying he'd hurt its feelings."

She was just like my dad in other ways, too. They both loved to play practical jokes, particularly on each other. Aunt Liv was a DJ at a local country Western station—Mustang Sally was her radio name. One time she announced on the air that Dad was trying to get in the Guinness World Records by buying up more boxes of Girl Scouts cookies than anyone on record. She gave out our address on the air, and by the end of the day, Girl Scouts were arriving at our house by the busload from all parts of the county.

Aunt Liv's life was like one of the sad country Western songs she played all day— She'd never met a cowboy who didn't eventually ride off without her. But she never gave up.

Miss Doodle made one last swipe at me through the cage, snagging my pant leg.

"Ouch!" I winced and then moved the carrier a safer distance away.

Aunt Liv propped herself up on an elbow on the bed. She wore long beaded earrings that swung back and forth. She clicked her tongue, and an entire herd of cats jumped up next to her. Aunt Liv was the local rescue mission for lost, abandoned, and abused cats. I suspected cats all over the country carried her address in their little kitty suitcases when they went out into the world. They had all been hiding until Miss Doodle was safely captured.

I pulled a small calico kitten on to my lap. She began to give my hand a complete wash and polish with her prickly tongue.

"Hey," Aunt Liv said, giggling as a tabby stood on its hind legs and tried to bat her earrings. "Remember the time your mom and dad went to New York and left you with me? And you got that nasty ear infection, and I had to put those drops in your ears?"

"Yeah," I cut in. "You chased me all over the house until I wore out and hid in the closet."

"Uh-huh—and you absolutely refused to come out!"

"Well, I finally did," I said.

She rolled her eyes at me. "Not until I agreed to pay you a dollar to do each ear."

I sighed and leaned against her. "You would have made a terrible mother, Aunt Liv, but you were always a great babysitter."

She kissed the top of my head. "Thanks, sugar. And you are the best niece in the universe. Your mom and dad are very lucky to have you—so is our little Jack Man," she added.

I put my hand next to hers, palm to palm. My hand looked like an oven mitt compared to hers. But I never felt self-conscious with Aunt Liv about anything. She always made me feel like everything about me was perfect. "I miss Dad so bad," I said. "Have you heard from him?"

She pulled a kitten off her back. "Not for a bit," she said, her voice giving me a tiny sidestep.

I tried to speak but couldn't get out what I wanted to say. I wasn't even sure yet what I wanted to ask her. I peeled at a hangnail until she grabbed it and kissed my fingers.

"What's up, Mace?"

I stared into her eyes, searching for a clue, searching for anything she might know. Then the blurt— "Aunt Liv, is Mom going to divorce Dad?"

She tilted her head at me, first to one side and then the other side. *Trying to buy some time*, I thought. "What makes you ask that?"

"Something's not right. He's never stayed away this long before."

"Have you talked to your mom about it?"

"I haven't asked her if they're getting a divorce, if that's what you mean." I pulled my knees up under my chin and then ducked my face behind them while I spoke. "She's always so busy with work, or Jack, and whenever I bring Dad up, she says the same thing: 'Your father is very busy with some very important work right now.' She's like a broken record!"

"Well?" Aunt Liv asked.

My irritation with Mom was like a hornet, and once it got away from me, I lost control of it. I couldn't sit still anymore. I got up and buzzed around the room. "Dad's always been busy with 'important work,' but he's always found time to come home. I think he probably doesn't want to come home because she always nags at him, and to her, nothing he does is ever right!"

I paused at her bookcase and picked up my favorite picture of her and Dad from when they were kids. They were sitting on the green stools at Nana's, drinking enormous milk shakes. Dad had a big dark gap in his smile where he was missing teeth.

Aunt Liv waited, silent.

"I don't think she loves Dad anymore," I said in a rush, all the words run together like a long snake that had been waiting to get out.

Aunt Liv pulled me back onto the bed next to her. She smoothed out the shoulders of my shirt and gave me a squeeze. "Macy, I know it's hard to be a kid and understand what's happening with your parents. I remember how that feels." She paused. "I do know your mom and dad love each other, and you, very much."

"Seems like Mom only loves Jack these days," I said, and then felt embarrassed by how pathetic that sounded.

"You know," Aunt Liv said, her voice soft, "when Gum was born, I was four, and I was so thrilled. It felt like about five Christmases all rolled into one." She picked up a comb from her bedside table and dragged it through my hair. "But when I started to see how Nana looked at him, like she had just given birth to the Messiah—" She faded off a moment, remembering. "Well, I turned into one of those really wicked characters from the fairy tales. I started plotting Gum's death!"

"Really? You wanted to *kill* Dad?" I asked, amazed and relieved. My occasional what-if-there-were-no-Jack fantasies worried me.

"Oh, absolutely! Anything to get rid of him. I got an idea from some story Nana was reading to me about this baby in a tree that gets carried away by this big old bird. Remember that giant old oak tree we had out back at Nana's?"

"The one with the tire swing?"

"Mmm-hmm. That's the one! Well, I figured if I could just climb up high enough with him, this bird from the story would swoop down and pick him up. I even told Nana I was going to do it!"

"What'd she say?" I said.

Aunt Liv chuckled. "She took me out back and looked up at the tree with me. Had me point to the branch where I was going to take him. Then she told me to make a muscle."

"She told you to make a muscle?"

"Yep! And I was very nervous and made the best one I could. Nana gave it a good squeeze and then nodded, all serious. Told me that I'd need to wait until I was six before I was strong enough to climb that high while carrying a baby."

A smile found my mouth.

"And then, of course, by the time I was six, I was pretty crazy about him. Wouldn't let anyone lay a hand on my baby brother."

"I know," I sighed. "Jack drives me insane, always following me around, getting into my stuff, but I love the little stinker."

"And you do see how he looks at you, don't you?"

Like I was his personal superhero. It made it so hard to stay mad at him. "Yeah." I grew quiet.

She hooked my hair behind my ear—just like Switch had done—where it fell over my face.

"Your mom's having a hard time right now, sugar. You might want to give her a break. She's got the world's busiest little boy, a very sad girl missing her dad, and an enormous job taking care of lots of other people's kids—"

"And no husband around to help her," I added.

"Well, right, not around right now," she agreed, her voice full of regret and . . . something else that I could feel and hear but couldn't quite get.

I gave her a long look. I adored Aunt Liv for a million reasons, but one of them was that every now and then, I could see Nana looking at me right through her eyes. I swallowed around the small hot stone in my throat.

She laid her forehead on mine a quiet second, and then she looked cross-eyed into my eyes. Which always made us giggle.

She gave me a quick peck on the lips. "Okay, you!" she said, revving up. "We've got a kitty to deliver, and then I owe you one Super Stellar Galaxy Cheeseburger Combo!" She pulled a soft sweater over her head, which muffled whatever she was saying about the new cute night manager at the Galaxy Burger. "Just give me five minutes in the little cowgirls' room, okay?"

"Take your time," I said, pulling off all the kittens that clung to me like burrs. I just remembered I hadn't done part of what I wanted to come here for. I had a short but serious snoop to do.

I ducked into her home office and eased back the roll top on her desk, keeping one ear cocked for the bathroom door opening. I made a mental apology to her and began rummaging through her private things. I had to believe she would do the same thing if she were in my shoes. She had a ton of letters and bills piled up on her desk, and a very old cup of coffee that had grown what looked like a mushroom on its top surface. I scootched the mug to the back.

There was a large pile of contest and sweepstake entries and various other junk mail, and I quickly scanned through it all, looking for Dad's familiar handwriting anywhere. I had a crazy hope I'd find a letter he'd written to Aunt Liv, explaining why he wasn't coming home. The two of them had always been really close. I couldn't imagine he would keep anything from her. Of course, he'd probably email her or call her, not write a letter.

I sighed. Nothing.

My eyes lit on a pile of phone bills, and I grabbed

the top one. Looked like last month's bill. I dug through it until I got to the long-distance-calls page. I took a quick look around the door to make sure Aunt Liv hadn't come out. I scanned the list of calls. She had four calls to Los Robles—long, expensive ones. Looked like once a week, too. I turned back the page of her wall calendar and compared the dates. All the calls to Los Robles were on Saturdays, all at around three p.m.

I grabbed a pen and jotted down the number on the inside of my hand. The number was familiar. Very familiar, like maybe one I'd just studied less than two hours ago at the library.

If I wasn't mistaken, it was the number to the Los Robles Department of Veterans Affairs.

Dear Mr. Jimenez,

The Fourth Thing About Me: here is something that I don't like: C-H-A-N-G-E! You know that big sign on the interstate, when you first drive into Constant? It reads: "Welcome to Constant. Where the Good Life Never Changes." That's 100 percent not true. The "good life" changes all the time in Constant! Just this week they cut down that giant magnolia tree in front of the library! The Dairy Queen went out of business a few months ago, and they turned it into a computer store. On a hot summer day, I want a Blizzard, not a surge protector.

Everything in my life that was good has changed. My grandmother died, a dirty rat stole her shop, my dad is going to miss my birthday, and I don't even get to go to the same school as my best friend.

If everything in your life is good right now, Mr. Jimenez, all I can say is you better watch out. "Welcome to Constant. Where the Good Life Gets You Clobbered." I am thinking of having a T-shirt made with that written on the front of it. If you agree with me, I could order one for you too. My dad wears XL. What size do you wear? Did you start practicing your push-ups yet?

Yours very sincerely,
Macy L. Hollinquest

PS My aunt Liv is a DJ at KCOW radio and isn't married or dating anyone. She tried to find you on Match.com, in case you're single. I'm supposed to find out if you are. And if you like country music.

CHAPTER EIGHT

om and Jack were crashed out together on the couch when I got home. Mom's work files were scattered over the coffee table, which was also covered in baby snacks, tiny army tanks, and sticky-finger marks. Jack was lying on top of my mom, like he'd won the last round. She obviously had been trying to work before Jack and his army had invaded. I pulled the glasses off her nose and folded them carefully. I studied her face a moment. I hated how sometimes I loved my mother so much it made my heart just ache, and other times the sight of her alone was enough to make me want to slam every door in the house.

I tried to clean up the table just a bit, so she wouldn't wake to such a mess. I scooped up the soggy pieces of cookie, and a banana half that had been

✳ ✳ ✳ ✳

mutilated. Jack was teething again and was gumming on anything he could get his hands on these days.

I closed her laptop and stacked her files together. I wasn't ever supposed to look at her work papers. It was a major rule in our house. It was in case I knew any of her delinquent kids. I'd asked her the other day if she knew a kid named Switch, and she said she didn't. I'd gotten the feeling it was the real truth and not the I-can't-tell-you-the-truth-for-your-own-good truth. Mostly the kids I knew were so tired from sports and stuff we didn't have time to make any trouble. Well, except for me tomorrow. Lying to just about everyone and taking a trip out of town without permission put me right up there with all of Constant's juvies.

Jack snorted in his sleep, startling me. My hand knocked a plastic cup of grape juice over onto a stack of papers. *Dang!* I looked around for a napkin or something to wipe with, but there wasn't anything. I picked up the papers and ran into the kitchen, trying to balance the pool of juice before it spilled onto the floor. Grabbing a paper towel, I did my best to blot the juice off the top sheet. She was going to kill me! It was something from the Everest County Juvenile Court, and it looked important. It had a bunch of kids' names on it—with "Last Known Address" and "Date Fled Jurisdiction." I wasn't really reading it; I was mopping it. But the names were beaming up into my brain, whether I wanted them to or not.

None of them rang a bell with me, anyhow. But I wondered where all these kids had fled to. *Jillian Lee Scoates* . . . Where are you? *Terrance Rose Jacobs*— Geez, what kind of parents names a guy Terrance *Rose*?

"Oh! You're home." Mom padded in barefoot behind me, scaring my wits right into the next state. She looked over my shoulder. "What are you doing with my files?" she asked, reaching for them.

"Oh, uh, I was just trying to clean up the coffee table for you, and I spilled some juice on them. Sorry!"

She took the towel out of my hand and looked down at the top sheet and then at me. "It's okay, honey, but you didn't—"

"I didn't read it, swear!" I said guiltily.

"I trust that if you did see anything by accident, you'll keep it confidential, right?" She sorted through the soggy stack, assessing the damage.

"Yeah, yeah, I know—"

She covered a yawn. "S'cuse me! Oh, Twee called a while ago. I asked her what time she was coming over to take care of Jack. She said six thirty. I told her that seemed really early and hardly necessary. She asked me if I'd talked to you tonight. What's up?"

I quickly collected the dirty dishes from the counter and turned on the hot water full blast. So it was nice and loud.

"I'm going out with the Green Angels in the morning. Real, real early. I need to be at the Elks Club parking lot by seven," I said. Fortunately, I'd had a Green Angel in my history class last year who blathered constantly about their comings and goings.

Mom crossed her arms and leaned up against the sink. About seven different expressions crossed her face. I watched her out of the corner of my eye as she opened and closed her mouth a couple times. She was clearly trying to decide if I had recently gone insane. She pretty much knew that the only thing that would get me up before eight on a summer morning would be a house fire. And like Twee said, recycling is not high on my list of things I'm famous for.

"Well, I think that's great! You know how I feel about recycling." She reached over and rubbed the small of my back. "If you're going to be so nice as to do the dishes *and* clean up the environment, at least let me pack you a lunch." She pulled open the fridge and studied its interior. "Turkey and Cheddar, okay? We're out of Swiss."

"Whatever," I mumbled, shutting off the water.

"Did you and Aunt Liv have a good time?" she asked.

"Guess so. We dropped Miss Doodle off at the vet, and then we went to Galaxy Burger." I paused, and then added, "And we talked about Dad."

Mom got very busy inspecting the lettuce. She did this to me all the time now. The minute the subject of Dad came up, she'd go mute. Lately, I kept throwing out his name just to prove my point to myself.

"Mom, how come you won't let Dad come home anymore?"

She whirled around, her cheeks bright. "'How come I won't let Dad come home anymore?'"

Major mother stalling technique #3: repeat child's question.

"How come you won't let Dad come home anymore?" I said louder, much louder.

She closed the fridge door very carefully, as if she didn't want to wake its contents. "Did Aunt Liv tell you that?"

"No!" I said. "It's what I think! Dad used to come home every month, and now he doesn't anymore. I know he still loves me and he still loves Jack, so it must have to do with you. Why do you always have to be so mad at him?"

Mom put her hands on my shoulders and gently

steered me to the breakfast nook. It was an old booth we'd taken out of Nana's that Dad had set up in the kitchen. It was where we had most all our family meetings. "Okay, Macy, let's talk," she said, trying to be calm, but I could hear the hurt and anger riding the edge of her voice.

She drew a deep breath. "When you're a little older—"

"When I'm a little older?" I interrupted, my voice sharp. "I still won't understand why you don't love him anymore!"

"This has nothing to do with anyone's love for another."

"Well, what does it have to do with, then?" I felt breathless, like I was hiking where the air was too thin.

She gave me a long look. And then looked down and studied her hands a moment.

I hated that I was hurting her, but I couldn't seem to stop myself. "Are you going to di*vorce* him?"

She reached for my hands across the table, but I yanked them away and tucked them under my legs.

"Well, are you?" I pressed.

"Your dad," she explained in a slow, quiet voice, like she was talking to someone who had an IQ of minus ten, "is working on a special project that is extremely important, and whether you choose to believe it or not, he is not able to come home right now."

"I am sick to death of hearing you say that!" I said, slapping a hand on the table, making the salt and pepper shakers jump. "Dad would not miss spending my birthday with me unless there was something else going on. The only thing that has ever kept him away before was the *war!*"

Mom took my hand and covered it with soft hands. Her face, usually smooth, looked rumpled, like a T-shirt left sitting in the dryer too long.

"Macy—" she started.

I pulled my hand back. "I know there's something else going on; why won't you admit it?"

She made a teepee with her fingers and then covered her mouth a moment. "The 'something else' is that he can't leave this project, honey. I'm afraid this is more important than anything right now."

What felt like a swarm of angry bees flew around inside my head. "I don't believe you! You just don't want him home, and he knows it!"

She shook her head as her eyes filled up with tears. "That's not true."

"It IS true," I yelled. "Ever since Dad got out of the service, you've been acting funny. You're always mad at him, and don't try to tell me you're not! I'm not stupid. I can smell it all over the place."

She tried to press the tremble out of her lips with her fingers. She nodded. "You're right. I have been mad at him a lot. But that doesn't mean I'm mad at you, and it doesn't mean I don't care about your father."

She pulled a napkin out of the dispenser on the table and wiped her eyes. I looked away from her face, noticing all of a sudden what she was wearing. She had on a Caffeine Nana's T-shirt.

"Why are you wearing *his* shirt?" I asked, my voice sharp as a shard of glass.

She looked down, startled. "Oh! This isn't Dad's shirt; it's mine. Chuck gave it to me a while back."

"I know it's not Dad's shirt! I meant why are you wearing Chuck's shirt?"

Mom rubbed her forehead. "Why are we talking about Chuck? This isn't about him."

"Of course it's about him! Ever since he stole Nana's coffee shop, our family has been falling to pieces. Why won't you admit that?"

Mom sat back in the booth, as if the force of what I said took her by the shoulders and pushed her back. "Honey, Chuck did not steal Nana's from us, and he has nothing to do with our family. I know you've got this grudge against him, but if you'd give him half a chance—"

"If I gave him half a chance, he'd probably try to move in *here*, too. Gee, he could just take Dad's place. Then he'd have it all!" My voice cracked at the end, all crazy-like.

Mom got up to come over to my side, but I shot out from the end of the booth. She tried to reach for me, but I backed away from her. "I don't want to talk to you anymore," I said.

I whooshed my way out the kitchen door and into the living room. I nearly mowed right over Jack, who was staggering into the kitchen, dragging his blankie. I leaned over and scooped him up. He was limp and warm, like a little bear cub. I buried myself in his baby sweetness while I tried to calm myself. I whispered into his tiny ear as I carried him to his bed. "It's time for me to go get Daddy, Jack. I'm bringing him back where he belongs. That's an official Big Sister Promise. You can take that to the bank!"

CHAPTER NINE

The left wing of the old jet was cool and damp in the early morning air. I crawled out on all fours to Switch's "mailbox," trying not to slip and break my neck before the day had barely started. Sure enough, there were some initials scratched into the metal near the flap. Was it an *S* or a *T*? Then an *R* and a *J*. I realized I didn't even know his last name. Everybody always just called him Switch. But under the initials was a pasted skateboard decal. No mistaking this was his post office box.

I unfolded the note I'd scrawled before I left the house. I'd used my left hand to make my writing look bad, like a little kid's. Like Buster's might look. I needed to throw Switch off track a bit. I'd die of guilt if he found the dog while I was in Los Robles. Twee

* * * * *

would never forgive me. Well, she would, but I could never forgive myself.

I read the note over one more time.

Deer Switch, I remembird something else. The van that took that dog was a pizza deelivary van. I think it wus frum pizza world. You shuld check them out. They took the dog I bet. Sum cute girls were asking me queshtons but I didun say nothing.

Your frend Buster

I folded the note back into tiny squares and shoved it into the opening. Then I swung myself over the side of the wing and dropped into the grass below. Hopefully, he'd spend the day chasing down dead-end pizza vans and end up with nothing more than pepperoni breath. I hitched my backpack up over my shoulders, grinning at the thought.

I took a gamble that Ginger was one of those old people who got up early every day—the kind who have their lawn edged and their car washed before eight a.m. I had to talk to her, alone, without Twee. And this was my only chance.

Last night I dragged one of Mom's psychology books into bed with me and looked under the section called "Gerontology," which I knew was about old people. I did a report on it last year in school. About how we forget to appreciate our elders and how important grandparents are to kids.

I had an idea that Ginger might be one tomato short of a BLT, and I wanted to find out if there was a way you could tell for sure. The book listed some questions you could ask to find out if someone had dementia, but I didn't have a clue how I could work the questions into an ordinary conversation. Like, you could ask them what year it was, or see if they could name the last five presidents, going backwards. Bad personal hygiene could be a symptom, and so could loss of strength and flexibility. But those could be from other medical problems you get when you're old.

Old age sure was complicated. I read a bunch of "case studies," too, but I didn't read about anybody who had a kitchen full of dog food and no dog.

I checked my watch. I still had forty-five minutes to spare before I had to be at the bus station. I wheeled my bike up to her door quietly. The kitchen window was open, and I could smell coffee. That was a very good sign.

The door pulled open wide just as I raised my fist to knock, surprising us both.

"Oh! Lacy!" she said with a start.

"It's Macy," I said. "Hi—um, sorry to disturb you!"

Ginger was obviously fresh out of the shower, with her hair still wet and neatly braided down the back. Five points for personal hygiene.

"I was just going to fill the bird feeders," she said, shifting a sack of birdseed on her hip. "Want to help me?"

"Sure!" I said, trying to take the bag from her.

"Oh, no, honey, I've got it," she said, smiling. "Gotta keep my muscles in shape."

Okay, she's still strong, and she's agile, I thought. No big deal that she'd called me Lacy. I couldn't ever remember the name of her missing dog. I followed her around the outside of the house to the side gate leading to the back, and sucked in my breath. Ginger had grown the Garden of Eden in her backyard. It was even more spectacular than the front yard. It smelled ripe with fresh fertilizer, and nearly every inch was covered with thick green grasses and enough flowers to cover the entire Rose Parade. I almost had to shade my eyes from so many bright colors. All along her fence were rosebushes with flowers the size of softballs.

"This is amazing," I said.

"Thanks, Macy," she said, setting down the bag of birdseed. "I used to do this all myself. Now, I have to have some help with it."

"The White House has lovely gardens too," I said. "Have you ever been there?"

"A couple of times," she said as she pulled down the tray from a bird feeder.

"Really!" I said, my voice way too enthused. "How interesting! Who were the presidents in office when you were there—both times?"

Truly lame, I thought.

She stopped what she was doing and gazed off into the distance a moment. "Let's see . . . Abe Lincoln the first time, and then— Oh, what was his name? Oh, yes! James Madison, the second trip." She looked at me with a big smile.

My heart sank a little. I didn't want her to be crazy. I really liked her.

"I'm kidding, honey!" she said. "I was there during the Carter and Reagan administrations. Just pulling your leg a bit."

"Ohhhh!" I said, full of relief.

She finished filling the bird feeder and then sat down next to a bed of hot-pink flowers. She patted the ground next to her. "Come sit with me while I do a bit of weeding. What's on your mind? I'm very happy to see you this morning, but I get the feeling you're here to ask me some more questions. I don't want to keep you from that with my silliness."

"Right," I said. "The more information I have, the better I can help find your dog."

And then, of course, I couldn't remember one single question I'd wanted to ask her. She waited in respectful silence for a while, pulling weeds and clipping back blossoms that had gotten brown and crispy.

"So how do you know Chuck?" I finally blurted.

She looked up at me, quizzical. Then took a deep breath. "He's good man, Macy. He's been a very good friend to me. I know you're not overly fond of him, though."

"He stole and ruined my nana's coffee shop."

She nodded. "I know it seems ruined to you, but—" She broke off and then shook her head.

"But what?" I asked when it seemed she wasn't going to continue.

"Well," she said, carefully picking off a small snail from a young bud. "I wonder if the 'ruined' part is just the plain fact that your grandmother isn't there anymore."

I swallowed.

She studied the snail up close. "Losing someone you love changes everything. It is really quite impossible to absorb. Sometimes you need to stay really mad about it for a while. Just so you can survive the shock of it all." She set the baby snail down on the brick border away from her flowers. She drew a deep breath and looked off in the distance again. Started to speak, but then just cleared her throat hard instead.

Unfolding her legs she stood up, and brushed her pants off. She reached a hand out for me, pulled me up next to her. "But if you stay mad, you stay alone. And when you've lost someone, that's the loneliest place in the world to be." She gave my hand a slow squeeze and then let it go.

I felt that prickling between my shoulder blades that I felt the first time I met her. "Do you feel alone?" I asked, my voice small.

She put an arm across my shoulders and waved out at her garden with her hand shovel. She lifted her shoulders and then dropped them. "I'm trying to fill it up best I know how, Macy."

I looked out at the row after row of flowers in her yard and thought of the rows of dog food in her kitchen. I could see how she was trying to fill up every square inch of empty space in her life. So far, I kept all my empty spaces full of mad. That's what I grew in my garden.

"Come inside with me a minute, will you? I have something for you."

I brushed the knees of my pants as I followed her

into the house. She opened the door to her darkroom and motioned me in. It was very cool inside, and the light was eerie. But I liked it.

"Do you remember the story the local paper did on your grandmother when she celebrated the thirty-fifth anniversary of her café?"

"Sort of," I said. "Mom has it somewhere. Why?"

"I remembered last night that I took the pictures for that, and wondered if I still had the negatives." She placed what looked like a blank sheet of paper into a metal tray full of liquid. With tongs, she carefully dunked the paper, so it stayed below the liquid.

"Now, keep your eyes on it," she said.

I leaned over the tray and watched as the paper slowly began to change. Shadows started to appear, some lighter and some darker, and then little by little, the outline of a face. The eyes came first and held me, and then the mouth and familiar crow's-feet around the eyes. Nana emerged like a ghost from the past, but not a ghost at all. The hundred details of her began to fill in then. A whole life lived on that face. I could hardly breathe. She looked alive.

And there was something else. There in the shadows of the shop, barely visible over Nana's shoulder, a man in a white T-shirt.

My father.

"I'd wanted to use this picture for the piece in the newspaper, but she didn't care for it. Said her hair was a mess, and she wanted to just use the photo of the front of the café." Ginger laughed, remembering. "She told me that it had weathered the years better than she had."

"You—you knew her?" I said in a small voice when I could finally trust myself to speak.

"I wouldn't say I 'knew' her, but I had the pleasure of meeting her. I liked her. She was a straight shooter."

"I think this is the best picture anyone ever took of her," I said, full of awe. "It's how she actually looked, you know? Can I really have it?"

"Of course. I made it just for you."

As she looked at me, I fought an urge to hug her as we stood in that dark private space. But we weren't alone. We were sharing it with Nana and—only I knew—with my dad.

Feeling shy, I stuck out my hand. "Well, thanks a lot. I really love it."

Ginger took my hand and squeezed it. "You are so welcome. But you need to leave it with me to dry, okay?" She paused a moment and then added, "Twee tells me it is your birthday in a few days. Would you allow me to photograph you two as a birthday gift? The two of you are quite special together."

"I'm *not*—" I started, and then softened my voice. "I'm not celebrating my birthday. At least not yet. You don't need to give me a present."

She regarded me a moment but didn't ask me any questions or interrogate me. She just left it alone. I loved that about her.

"Well, take it from an old dame. When you're older, you'll appreciate having a picture of the two of you to remember this summer. You'll be all grown up before you know it. Perhaps you'll allow me to take photos to simply celebrate two best friends."

With a gulp, I wondered if it would be our last summer together. I prayed Twee would even be speaking to me next week. If I was so lucky, this would be the last double cross I would ever do of her. *That*, I swore on my nana.

My resolve melted like an Eskimo Pie on a hot spit at the sight of the express bus to Los Robles. I bit down hard on my lip and checked my watch. Just in time. I handed my ticket to the bleary-eyed clerk in the window, who ripped it down the middle and handed me half. She pointed to the bus.

I had made myself stay up real late last night baking cookies, hoping I'd be so tired I'd fall right to sleep on the bus. Yeah, right.

I tiptoed on to the hulking metal thing, like there might be a land mine under any one of the steps. Then I stood tall in the aisle, breathing deeply.

Took two steps. Stopped. *Inhale.*

Four steps. Wiped the sweat off my upper lip. *Exhale.*

Six steps. Pictured how glad my dad would be to see me. *Inhale.*

Eight steps. A wave of dizzy made my knees buckle, and I caught myself on a seat. *Steady, steady.*

Ten steps and then no stopping until the end. I moved quickly with stiff, short strides, my eyes on the black rubber aisle runner.

And then on two big long feet in holey socks.

I caught my breath at the sight of Switch camped out on the long backseat—sound asleep, curled up like a little mouse. A crumpled paper bag was halfway shoved under the seat along with his skateboard, a carton of chocolate milk, and some old curly French fries.

His watch beeped and his eyes flew open. He rubbed his head and then caught sight of me staring at him like he was some kind of alien.

"Hey!" he said, reaching for his chocolate milk. He took a deep swig, his eyes never leaving me. "What are you doing here? Need a place to hurl again?" He wiped his mouth on his sleeve.

"No!" I said, waving my ticket in his face. "I'm going to Los Robles—to see my dad." I bit down on my lip, hard. My big secret just leaped right out of my mouth like it wasn't mine to keep.

"Cool." Switch started packing up and putting everything into his bag. At least he was tidy. Some boys would have left all their food junk on the floor.

"Are *you* going to Los Robles?" I asked, trying hard not to sound too interested.

"Naw, I was just hanging out, catching some Zs."

I pointed my head over in the direction of the station. "What if you got caught?"

He shook his head. "Not too worried about that. I know the graveyard guy inside. He's cool. He's a skater too," he said, his foot finding his wheels below him. "Sometimes I help him clean out the bus or inside the terminal for a couple bucks." Switch studied me a minute. "So, what's your story? You get on the bus the other day, lose a load, and leave. Now, you're back. I'm no shrink, but you got some problem about going to see your dad or something?"

My cheeks flushed. "No. I *love* my dad."

"You're not one of those girls who eat and then puke it up on purpose, are you? Because that is so lame."

I stared at my feet a moment, feeling a ridiculous

urge to confess. "No— It's just that— Well, buses make me puke."

"Can't your mom drive you to your dad's?" he asked, puzzled.

I gnawed the inside of my cheek. "She doesn't exactly know I'm going."

"Oh," he said. "This is getting interesting." He pulled me down next to him, close. "Give it up."

The pulse point in my temple started beating like a tiny drum.

"You running away?" he asked.

I shook my head. "No. I just need to see my dad real bad."

Switch looked over at me sideways. "You know, I could take you."

I guffawed. "What? On your skateboard?"

"I got wheels," he said, giving me a long, slow smile. He had really white teeth, and this loopy scar at the corner of his mouth, like a fish that had once been hooked. I wondered how he got it.

A uniformed driver hopped aboard and picked up his clipboard. Switch scootched down in his seat. The driver turned over the ignition, gave it some gas. And then revved the engine a few times, like he was going to race it in the Indy 500 or something.

A cloud of smoke billowed up. My mouth felt like

it was filled with exhaust. I might as well have been under the bus, sucking on the tailpipe. I swallowed and licked my lips.

Switch looked me over. "I'll make you a deal. Go turn in your bus ticket. They'll give you cash back for it. You give me half for gas; you take half for snacks on the way. What do you say?"

I couldn't say much of anything.

"Oh, man, you're going all green on me! C'mon." Switch grabbed his board and sack in one arm, and me in the other. Dragged me down the aisle.

Sweat ran down both my legs, and it felt like I was wearing cement boots. Switch looked back at me. "Hang on—almost there."

My head grew heavy and stupid. A strong arm came around my waist, dragged me the rest of the way. I don't remember getting out. Next thing I knew I was sitting with my head pushed down between my legs.

"Stay!" Switch barked.

No problem, I thought.

Moments later something icy cold was pressed against my neck. My eyes rolled back into their proper places, and the dancing lights finished their sideshow.

"Kid, you weren't joking about hating the bus!"

Switch's voice was close and teasing next to my ear.

I grabbed the cold thing he was pressing against my neck. It was a can of soda. I rolled it against my face. I tried to look at him, but his face was too close, and there were three of him.

He took the can from me and popped the lid. "Here, drink. You could use some caffeine."

I took a long swig, trying to get the world back into focus. I stared at the line of people getting on the bus.

"So, what'ya think?" he asked. His eyes swept my face. "You gonna get on, or you gonna take me up on my deal?"

The driver pulled the last ticket, checked his watch, and double-checked the luggage storage. Then he looked over at me. "Coming, miss? Time to pull out."

I wiped my sleeve across my forehead. I tried to imagine myself getting back on, settling in a seat, even saw myself waving good-bye to Switch. Then the driver would have to give it some gas, and we'd lurch out into traffic. Before I knew it we'd be tearing down the freeway toward Los Robles.

My stomach seized up into a ball of snow. I stuck my head back between my legs.

Switch patted the top of my head. "Naw, go on," he told the bus driver. "She's with me."

"Hey," Switch said, leaning in. "Let me take you, okay? You need to see your dad real bad? I'm your man. I'll get you there, no problem."

I sat up and dragged a deep breath of fresh air. Gave him a long sideways look. Quickly counted up how many weeks I'd probably get grounded for this. Weighed that against not seeing my dad. Weighed it against Jack growing up in a broken home.

"I'll go turn in my ticket," I said.

Barely an hour later I was trudging back to Jet Park. Sort of like déjà vu, but without the mystery. Switch told me to meet him here while he went to deliver his newspapers and get his wheels. Said he could get there faster on his board. We'd had a short conversation about his age, and the fact that he didn't actually have a license. He explained that was only a technicality, as he'd had the class and drivers' training. What was most important was that he knew how to drive.

Oh, boy, would my mom love to get her hands on that argument. She'd pound it into holiday mincemeat. Her whole world was technicalities, making sure every kid in the county followed the very letter of the law. And living under the same roof with Mrs. Probation Pants meant that whatever I did always got serious scrutiny.

But, like Switch said, some good things didn't fit under the law. We had stopped at a small market near the bus station to pick out some snacks for our trip. While I was paying for our stuff, I saw Switch slip a cigar into one of the "free" newspapers he was holding. He just smiled at me when I'd looked at him shocked, and then he cruised out of the store, like he didn't have a care in the world. I left a whole dollar in the "take a penny, leave a penny" tray, hoping that would cover the price of a cigar.

"Are you *crazy*?"

"Will you relax? It's for one of my old guys on my paper route. He loves a good stogie. Not that he'll ever smoke it," he added with a grin. "He'll just gum it to death all day."

"But I could have paid for it!" I sputtered.

"I know, but why should you? It's not for you, and it's not for me." Switch just jumped up on his board with a giant clack. "If I can make the day nicer for someone, I'm going to do it. So, arrest me," he'd said, holding his wrists out for handcuffs. His eyes locked on my face, teasing.

Twenty minutes later I was busying myself with repacking my backpack to take my mind off my superterrible new plan to get to Los Robles.

I popped open the lid on the tin of macaroons I'd

brought my dad. Took a deep whiff. They were his favorite treat in the world. I could hardly believe that in just a few hours I could be seeing him, and we'd be eating these very cookies together.

Mom seemed surprised that I was baking so late last night. I told her in a frosty voice that the Green Angels loved macaroons. I could tell she wanted to patch things up between us, but I wouldn't give her an inch. Not even a half inch.

The sidewalk under me rumbled, and a distant roar cut through the quiet morning. I looked overhead for a helicopter, shading my eyes from the sun. The rumble grew stronger, louder, and was moving toward Jet Park.

In the distance, but coming closer, Ginger's motorbike came barreling down Lincoln Drive. I whipped my head in all directions, looking for the white-haired boy on the skateboard—the boy who almost got creamed by this very motorbike just days ago.

The bike came to a quick, noisy stop just feet away from me. The driver tossed me a helmet and motioned toward the sidecar. Then flicked up the goggles and smiled at me.

"Come on! Let's go!"

I just stood there staring at him, my mouth the perfect flytrap.

"Get IN, or I'm leaving without you!" he shouted.

"YOU— You— You!" I could only sputter.

He revved the motor. "Okay, I'm leaving! And I've got all your cash, remember?"

Like a zombie, I pulled on the helmet. Stepped down into the small seat.

"Los Robles, here we come!" Switch whooped, gunning the gas.

And off we flew, looking *exactly* like my mother's worst nightmare.

CHAPTER TEN

If you ever find yourself being bounced and blown out of town in the sidecar of an old vintage motorcycle, you'll find out quick that the driver can't hear anything you are screaming at him. Especially important questions like—

"Are you *OUT OF YOUR MIND*?"

And "Do you *REALLY* think I am going to go ALL the way to Los Robles in *THIS* thing?"

Even my threats were lost to the wind. Like "If *YOU* don't pull over *RIGHT* now, I'm going to go up there and *RIP* your eyeballs right out of their *SOCKETS*!" Which I punctuated with a very, very bad cussword.

I continued to yell at him until my throat was ground meat. Just to make sure he wasn't just ignoring the hard questions, I tried screaming something else.

* * * * *

"YOU HAVE A GIANT HOLE IN YOUR JEANS AND I CAN SEE YOUR UNDERPANTS!"

But he just turned around, smiled, gave me a thumbs-up. Switch was having a swell time.

The only upside to this nightmare journey was that I was outside. I could breathe. I wasn't trapped inside an old, smelly bus. I was trapped outside an old, smelly bike.

Mile after mile the wind pounded me, parting my eyelashes and blowing my nostril hairs backward into my sinus cavity. After a while I couldn't yell anymore, and my eyes were too dry to keep open. My head started bobbing and weaving. I'd never sleep, though, not while my life was in the hands of Robin the Teenage Hood.

Miles later the smell of gasoline dragged me back. My head popped up, my neck stiff and sore. I shifted my helmet back onto my head, where it had slipped over my eyes. Licking sandpaper lips, I looked for Switch. He stood next to the gas pump, chowing down on a corn dog.

"Man, you were out!" He pointed his dog over at me. "Bite?"

I gave him a poisonous look and unfolded myself from the sidecar. Punched him hard in the arm and headed toward the bathroom.

"You might want to get some gratitude!" he called after me. "You're the one who wanted to go to Los Robles."

I turned on my heel and marched back to the bike. "I do want to go, but I'd like to get there alive!" I balled up my fist, punched him again, right in the same spot. It had to hurt.

Switch winced and rubbed his bicep. "Lighten up! We'll get there fine. Go— If you gotta use the restroom, get on it. I don't want to hang out here all day."

The bathroom was disgusting, and the mirror was no better than an aluminum cookie sheet. I pulled off my helmet to wash my face. I looked terrible. Not exactly how I'd hope to look on the day I was seeing my dad.

I sighed and wished Twee were here. She always made me feel better about everything. She could find the upside to nuclear disaster. I heard Switch gunning the bike outside, so I quickly splashed more water on my face. Hurried outside and pulled my helmet back on.

Switch handed me a giant grape Icee and smiled. "Better?"

I took a deep icy swig, and then another, and another. I ignored the deep stabbing pain in my right eye from the cold. It was worth it. I grabbed Switch's shoulder to turn him around. "Just tell me one thing. Did you steal this bike from Ginger?"

"Steal it?" he asked, giving me an annoyed look. "No way. I like the old girl."

He had completely evaded my question. "Switch! Does she know that you have her bike?"

He broke eye contact with me for just one flea-sized second, but I caught it.

"Of course she knows!" he said.

"'Of course she knows' as in she's calling the police right about now?"

"No! I wouldn't steal from an old lady—especially one that is off her nut."

"Ginger's not *off* her nut!"

"Yeah, she is—trust me. I can tell with old folks. Some of them seem perfectly normal when you first talk to them, and then the next minute, they think they are beekeepers. I just told her that I have a special driver's license for animal search and rescue, and she believed me."

"So you lied to her?"

"I told her what she needed to hear, so she wouldn't worry about me being on the bike. Big difference. I don't hurt old people. Ever."

I just stared at him, trying to decide if he was

really kind or one big fast-talker. Maybe he was both.

"You worry too much, kid," he said.

I drew a shaky breath. "Let's go," I said, looking away. I tried to fluff up the small seat pillow in the sidecar, but it was unfluffable. My butt was killing me. I heard something jingle under the pillow and lifted up a corner. The other side of the pillow was thick with white hair. Dog. I reached down and lifted the bright-blue collar, read the engraving on the tag: "Mr. McDougall. If lost, please call (555) 555-0190."

I studied it a minute and then wrapped the collar around my wrist twice. Switch tore out of the gas station, throwing me back in my seat. I righted myself and then rubbed Mr. McDougall's tag between my fingers, warming the metal. I pictured his face from all the photographs I'd seen at Ginger's. He really had one of those great dog faces—loyal, noble, and funny, all rolled up in one furry mug. I honestly wanted to find him. Ginger's face came to me then, and with it, an ache in my gut. The times when I was with Ginger, I couldn't tell which one of us the ache belonged to.

Whatever the case, I just wanted to make it go away. For both our sakes.

Okay, Mr. McDougall. Here's the deal. You help me find my dad today, and I'll get you and your mom back together. If you're anywhere around, I'm going to find you. Tomorrow, you have my undivided attention. Deal?

I rubbed the tag again on his collar to seal the deal. And swear I thought I heard a dog bark over the roar of the engine.

Hours later Switch and I tore into half-pound burgers at Los Robles Drive 'n' Dine, on the edge of town. I lathered my fries in thick ketchup and almost drooled on the table. Being on the open road all this time had made us ravenous.

By midmorning Switch had eaten all the snacks that I'd planned for lunch. He was the hungriest kid I ever met. But since I was at his mercy, I made it my mission to keep him fed and watered. The closer I got to Dad, the less important being angry at Switch seemed.

Switch cocked his head over at me. Nodded toward my hand gripping a drippy burger. "You got some big mitts, kid. Ever think of playing basketball?"

I choked down a large piece of meat. "I play soccer."

"That's cool. You any good?" he asked.

I took a long drink of soda. "I dunno. I do all right. My dad was a good soccer player when he was a kid."

"Your parents split up?"

I shook my head and then paused. "I'm not sure what they are right now. That's why I'm going to see

him. I have to figure it out. What about your folks?"
I asked, and then wished I could have grabbed the
question back. Not a great question for somebody
who lives in a foster home.

Switch unfolded his napkin and wiped each of his
fingers carefully. He was a very tidy eater for a boy. I
quickly wiped my mouth.

"Never knew my dad, really. He went off to fight
in Iraq and never made it back. He didn't die— He just
didn't come back to us." He shrugged like it didn't
matter, but I knew it did.

"He might as well be dead. I've got no respect for
a dude who leaves his wife and kids. He never even
sent money. My mom— She works a lot. Day and
night, sometimes. She ended up doing drugs, just so
she could keep up and stay awake. Ended up getting
busted for driving high with us kids in the car. So,
the county split us up. Sent me to foster care, and my
baby sister, Elle, got sent to this rich family who are
trying to adopt her. She's about your age, you know."

"Do you like your foster parents?" I asked.

Switch snorted. "Which ones?" He reached over
and jangled the dog collar still wrapped around
my wrist. "Nice bracelet, kid. Part of your new fall
fashion look?"

I crossed my arms against my chest. "It's Mr.

148

McDougall's collar. I found it under the pillow in the sidecar."

Switch grinned. "You really think you're going to find that old pooch, huh?"

"I'll find him before you do, that's for sure." I crumpled up my hamburger wrapper and sucked down a thick mouthful of mocha chip shake.

"I wouldn't count on that. I know every neighborhood, every park, every inch of sidewalk in that town. Heck, I've lived in half the houses in town. If that dog is still alive, *I'm* going to find him."

"Well, if you did," I said, "but you *won't*, what would you do with the reward money?"

Switch slunk down in the booth and got a dreamy look on his face. I could hear his skateboard beneath the table as he softly rolled it back and forth under his feet. I'd pretty much figured out that his board was his grown-up version of a blankie.

He sighed. "First I'd buy some new wheels— probably an Enjoi Whitey Panda." He pretended to pop a small wheelie under the table and grinned. "That is one *sweet* board! Then—" He stopped to munch a fry. "Oh, I don't know, I'd probably throw a big old party at Villa Rosa for the old folks there." He smiled at the thought. "I'd hire one of those old-timer bands, get some fancy restaurant to bring in food, maybe have it outside on the lawn. I'd get some waiters in tuxes to come serve everybody. You know, a real classy party."

I just shook my head. "The skateboard I would have assumed. A party at a nursing home? That I would not have guessed in a gazillion years."

He wiped carefully around his plate with his napkin and then shrugged. "A nursing home is even worse than foster care or a group home. And it's not like they did anything to deserve it. Other than getting old."

He smoothed the sides of his hair with the heels of his hands and tossed me one of his charming smiles, one meant to change the subject. "So, what would you do if *you* got the reward money?"

"Well, I'd be splitting it with Twee," I said right off. "She's saving for a trip to Vietnam. She wants to find some of her family, maybe her real parents if she can."

Switch nodded approvingly. "That's rip."

A busboy with bad skin and a wannabe skater attitude came by and filled up our water glasses. He looked at Switch like he'd just found Elvis. Even this many miles from his home turf, Switch gave off seriously cool vibes. Switch rewarded him with a quick jerk of his chin.

I took a deep breath. "And with my half, I'm putting it in my special account that my grandmother started for me when I was a baby. I'm saving up to get her coffee shop back from Chuck," I said. My mouth curled over his name, like I'd just licked the bottom of someone's shoe.

"You want to run a café?" he asked, surprised.

"Well, no—not really," I admitted. "But I don't want him to have my nana's coffee shop. He's just ruined it. Not to mention the fact that he pretty much stole it from my family."

"Chuck? Really? He seems like a righteous guy."

"Oh, he acts nice, all right. That's how he gets away with stuff. Charms everyone to death. After my nana died, he started nosing around, calling my mom all the time, sweet-talking her. My dad was a wreck, and Chuck knew it. He took total advantage of my mom and swindled the family out of the café."

"Didn't your dad know your mom was selling it?" he asked. "I mean it belonged to your dad, too, right? Your mom couldn't sell it behind his back."

"Yeah, sure, he told her it was okay," I said, decapitating a French fry with a quick snap of my front teeth. "My mom convinced him we needed the money for the new baby and everything. But I think it broke his heart that my mom sold the shop right out from under him. My dad gave up his career in the army and everything to run Nana's, but my mom wouldn't give him a chance."

Switch fiddled with his fork, watching me. "Well, at least Chuck kept it a coffee shop and kept her name in it. That's pretty respectful. And he's got that big picture of her up in there."

I swallowed. I didn't know he had kept her picture up. I hadn't been inside to see it.

"I mean, what if he changed it to a tire store named Chuck's Discount Whitewalls or something? That would have been tons worse."

I threw the fry down onto my plate. "Why are you sticking up for him? He's a snake."

He shrugged. "All I know is he's been pretty cool to me. Treats me good. Gives me free stuff sometimes."

I blushed, thinking of the hundreds of free Snow Whites I'd had "on the house" from Chuck.

"Well . . . you haven't heard everything," I said.

Switch raised a brow.

"I think he's in love with my mother," I blurted.

"Not a chance of that," Switch said matter-of-factly. He smiled and looked out the window. Then paled and froze.

I followed his gaze toward the motorcycle. Two highway patrol officers in enormous leather jackets were standing over it. And judging by the look of panic on Switch's face, I had a very bad feeling that the cops thought they'd just found themselves a stolen vehicle.

CHAPTER ELEVEN

Switch ducked way down into the booth until I could just barely see his eyes over the tabletop. "We gotta get out of here," he whispered.

I scootched down with him, my heart banging.

"Out the back," he mouthed. "Stay down, though."

I nodded dumbly.

"Ready?" he asked. "Let's go!"

"Wait! We haven't paid yet," I whispered.

Switch rolled his eyes at me and shot out of the booth. I pulled a wad of cash from my pocket and slapped it on the tabletop. I followed his path through the kitchen, keeping my head down, just waiting for someone to grab the back of my neck. Old Beach Boys music blared over the hum of dishwashers.

Switch eased open a rickety screen door and took

* * * * *

a quick look back for me. *"Hurry!"*

We closed the door quietly behind us and looked around the back. All clear.

"Now what?" I peeped.

"Shhh! Listen!" He froze.

Heavy boots crunched in the gravel to the left of us, along with the unmistakable sound of walkie-talkie static, coming closer.

"C'mon!" he said, and raced toward the Dumpster.

I sprinted after him and ducked behind the back of it with him. He peeked around the side.

"Quick, get in!" He grabbed me below my bottom and hoisted me up. I did an ugly swan dive right into the middle of Drive 'n' Dine's garbage. Switch landed smack on top of me. He muffled my yelp with a tight hand over my mouth and rolled off me.

"Don't-move-don't-make-a-sound," he said slowly into my ear. His breath was hot and tangy, like the hamburger he'd just inhaled.

Switch put his head down into my shoulder. He kept his hand over my mouth, like I might burst into song or start shouting any moment.

The screen door banged, and muffled voices came from the back of the restaurant. And a lot more footsteps kicking around in the gravel.

I peeled Switch's hand off my mouth and took

a gulp of air. Big mistake. It stank way, way bad in Dumpsterville.

Switch lifted his head and tried to listen to what they were saying. The music from the kitchen was too loud. But one of the cops kept talking into his radio. Switch looked at me a moment and then squinched up his face in pain. He put his mouth next to my ear again. "My board! I left it inside." He shook his head and muttered a cussword I would never repeat.

The screen door banged again, and it got quiet. The music cut off abruptly.

Switch shifted a bit in the pile of garbage. Then whispered the cussword again.

"Did you steal Ginger's bike?" I hissed.

He shook his head. "No! I already told you that."

"Then why are we hiding?"

He clapped his hand over my mouth again. "Shhh!"

The back door banged, and footsteps crunched toward us. We both froze, and I squeezed my eyes so tight I almost crushed my eyeballs.

A large box came over the top of the Dumpster and was set gently next to us. I opened one eye one-quarter to peek.

Busboy grinned down at Switch. "Brought your wheels, dude," he said softly, pointing to the box.

"Thanks, man!" Switch said. "Those cops gone yet?"

Busboy glanced over his shoulder. "Naw, they're back out front, nosing around your bike. Guess they wanted to ask you about it, what year it was and everything. When you guys split out back, they got, like, totally curious 'bout it, man. But Mac the owner was cool. Said you'd paid your bill and everything, so no sweat with him."

I elbowed Switch in his side.

"But if you leave your bike there all day, Mac'll probably tow ya."

"Thanks, bro'. Think we'll hang here for a while. Will you come tell us when the cops leave?"

"Course, man. But these guys are regulars. Good eaters, too. They're gonna knock back a couple of burgers and about a tank of coffee before they leave."

"Oh, great," I groaned. I pinched my nose shut a minute and took a deep breath from my mouth.

"Does the city bus come by here?" Switch asked.

Busboy nodded and motioned with his head over his shoulder. "Yea, every half hour or so. Picks up across the street about three blocks down."

The screen door squeaked open. "CAL-VIN! Quit squirrelin' around and get back in here, will you?"

Calvin reached into the Dumpster and rapped knuckles with Switch.

Switch waited until he heard the door slam again, and then sat up. He took a quick peek at his board in the box. As if to make sure Calvin hadn't accidentally brought him an inferior model.

I tried to rearrange myself into a semicomfortable squat. And tried hard not to look at what I was squatting on. But I couldn't help notice that it smelled like I was perched on top of a dead sea lion.

"What time is it?" Switch whispered.

"Ten after two," I said.

"Okay, here's the deal. We gotta split up for a while."

"What?"

"Look. You need to get to town and see your old man. I've got to stay with the bike. We can't take a chance of them towing it. I'll wait here. You grab the next bus."

I bit down hard on my lip. The bus? I didn't like the sound of this.

"Or you can walk into town instead," he said. "Which is gonna take most of the afternoon. Or you find a phone to call a cab. But that's probably going to cost twenty bucks or so." He paused. "It would be a pretty short bus ride. It's okay, Macy. You can do it."

I counted out the bills left in my pocket. Eleven

bucks. Looks like I'd accidentally left the waitress and Calvin about a fifteen-dollar tip. Between gas, snacks for the trip, and the load I'd just left inside, I'd pretty much blown my whole trip fund.

"Sorry," he said, watching me fold the bills back. "I've only got a couple of ones with me." He reached over and flicked a pickle slice off my arm. "It's like this. It's your deal, you call it. You can either take the bus now or hang out here until the cops leave, which could be another hour. And there's a chance we're gonna get towed even before they leave. Then we're *really* stuck. So, if you need to see your dad today, I'd take the chance and bust out of here now."

"How are we going to find each other later?" I asked.

"You're going downtown, right?"

I shrugged. "That's where I'm starting. It's the only address I have."

"There's a big music store right downtown called Boomtown Sounds. Meet me there at six o'clock," he said. "That'll give us two hours or so of good daylight to drive. If we haul it, we could be back by ten p.m. It'll be tight, but we can do it."

"What if I can't get there by six?" I said, a lot of worry and a little whine creeping into my voice.

"Then call Boomtown and leave a message there

for me. And if you get there, but I can't, I'll leave a message for you."

I nodded. I knew he was right. Time was wasting, and I couldn't sit in this Dumpster all day. . . . But splitting up? I didn't like it. Not one bit.

"Okay, then! Hit the road, kid."

I crawled up to the front of the Dumpster and took a quick peek over the top.

"Careful—don't let those cops see you!"

I crept to the far side, threw a leg up, and pulled myself over. Dropped to the ground as quietly as I could. Then ran like hell.

I folded in two over the top of the bus bench, my lungs heaving, like I was about to give birth to a calf. The "three blocks" to the bus that Calvin promised was only technically true. Three city blocks are very different from three small-town blocks I'm used to. Felt like I'd just run a marathon. As it was, I'd arrived only in time to suck up the fumes from the last bus, which, gauging from my watch, was the two-thirty p.m. run. Now, I was stuck another half hour.

A bearded guy wearing an old camo jacket in a wheelchair gave me a long look. I retucked my shirt, dumped some coffee grounds from the cuff on my shorts, and stared back at him. He didn't have any room to be looking down his nose at me. Neither of us was going to win a best-dressed contest any time soon.

He pulled a half-smoked butt out of an empty pack of cigarettes and lit it up. Took a deep drag from it and held it in. Then drank from a beat-up Styrofoam cup. I watched a moment, temporarily fascinated. He finally blew the smoke out in a big, stinky gust, stubbed the butt out with care, and put it away in his little empty pack.

"Um, excuse me," I said. "Was that bus that just left going to downtown Los Robles?"

Smokey ignored me.

I stepped up closer. "Sir, could you at least tell me if the next one coming is to Sixth Avenue? It's kind of an emergency that I get there."

He dumped out the rest of whatever was in his cup and dried it out carefully with a filthy bandana.

I crossed my arms and cleared my throat—neither of which inspired him to speak to me.

Looking at my watch, I did the math. I had just three and a half hours left to get downtown, find my dad, convince him to come home, and get back to Switch by six. Hopefully, provided we still had Ginger's bike, that would put us in Constance by ten p.m. If I was any later, my mother would have every cop in the state out looking for me.

I needed a back-up plan in case we didn't make the ten p.m. cutoff. I chewed the underside of my lip, and the knot of scar tissue that lived there from years of me gnawing at it.

I'd have to call Twee and come clean about this. She'd find a way to help cover for me. That is, after she killed me. I couldn't stand to think about the hurt that was going to set up camp on her face once I told her I'd come to Los Robles with Switch instead of her.

A large blue van pulled up at the bus stop, and Smokey rolled over to it. The driver eased out of the front seat and came around to open the side door. He looked like a California version of Santa Claus. He had a long white beard and an enormous Hawaiian shirt that stretched tightly across his middle. But it couldn't quite cover the large hairy canyon that served as his belly button.

He threw out a casual salute. "Hey, Jerry. What's up?"

Smokey grunted.

Santa cracked open the panel door and slung it back hard. He flipped a switch inside the back, and a wheelchair lift came out. He helped the guy roll his wheelchair on it.

My eyes locked on the writing on the panel door.

DEPARTMENT OF VETERANS AFFAIRS

SOUTHERN COLORADO HEALTH CARE SYSTEM

PROUDLY SERVING OUR NATION'S VETERANS

I licked my lips. Put my hand in my pocket.

Santa tucked his passenger in safely. "You going back to the Dom, Jer?"

Smokey nodded, looking straight ahead.

The driver grabbed the door handle with a beefy arm. "Let's go, then!"

"Wait!" I shouted, lunging for the doorway. I put my hand on the wheelchair. "Uncle Jerry! You said I could go with you this time. I've never seen your Dome, um, I mean your Dom! Mom can pick me up there later. Please, please, please?" I stepped up into the van next to him. Put my hand over his, quickly stuffing my last ten under his hand. "C'mon, Uncle Jerry, huh, what'ya say?"

He looked down at the ten and closed his hand tight. Flicked his eyes over me and held them for a split second. His eyes were deepwater blue, set against a white backdrop that was covered in red, bloody trails. I looked down a second and held my breath.

"Okay. Just don't bug me," he said in a voice all

163

raspy, probably because he never used it. He nodded at the driver and shrugged. "Dang niece."

I collapsed into the backseat and drew a long deep breath. "Thanks, man," I said.

"I *said*, don't bug me."

I waited at least five minutes after the van pulled away before I leaned forward. I didn't want to blow our deal, but I did need to get some direction here. "What's a Dom?" I whispered near the back of his head.

Silence.

"Where are we going?"

Nothing.

"Can you help me get to the Department of Veterans Affairs?" I asked. "It's on Sixth Avenue," I added helpfully. "Are we headed to Sixth Avenue?" I might as well have been talking to a corpse.

"Jerry, c'mon. I gave you ten bucks. That's going to buy you more cigarettes than you've seen in a long time."

He stuck a long, dirty finger in his ear and dug around, like he was looking for something. I leaned back and closed my eyes. Afraid to see what he might pull out, and worse yet, what he might do with what he pulled out.

After a couple of minutes, I started up again. "Look, my dad is a veteran too. He was in Iraq. I'm trying to find him. I gotta get to him this afternoon."

He turned his head slightly and peered at me with one mean eye. "Be quiet, or I'll open that door and shove you out."

"Could you just tell me one thing and I'll never speak again?" I pleaded. I took his silence as permission.

"Are we going to end up anywhere *near* Sixth Avenue?" I wasn't too familiar with downtown Los Robles. Usually, when Mom and me came, we went to the mall, which was north of town.

"Iraq was a field trip with big toys," he muttered. "'Nam was a war."

Not very helpful, but it was the most words he'd strung together yet. "So, I'm guessing you were in Vietnam?" I asked. "Do you ever go to the Department of Veterans Affairs on Sixth Avenue for reunions? You know, to look up old buddies or anything?" Truly lame, but I was desperate.

The van came to an abrupt stop. I whiplashed back against the seat and hit my head. "Sorry, guys!" Santa yelled over his shoulder.

I put my nose up to the grimy window and peered out. Looked like we were at some giant elementary school. Big redbrick buildings, lots of trees—a minicampus set back on a busy city street. It had a big playground with basketball courts. But no kids. Just a bunch of guys in wheelchairs. I eased out of the back of the van after "Uncle Jerry" got lowered out.

"So, is this your Dom?" I asked him.

He pointed a long, dirty fingernail at a sign across the sidewalk. It had a right-pointing arrow after the word "Domiciliary." Left arrow to "Medical Services." Right arrow to "Chapel." Left arrow to "Administration."

Jerry wheeled up to me. Grabbed my hand and stuffed a sweaty ten-dollar bill into it. Pointed his chin down the way toward the corner.

I shaded my eyes against the glare as I looked up at a very tall building, probably ten stories high. Read the sign etched in its side.

LOS ROBLES VA MEDICAL CENTER

I looked down at the bill in my hand, then back at him. "So is this—" I started.

"The Department of Veterans Affairs," he muttered, turning right and rolling himself down Sixth Avenue.

Dear Mr. Jimenez,

The Fifth Thing About Me: I come up with sensational ideas. Since my mom doesn't want me to stay back a grade, what if Twee skips a grade and comes to Kit Carson with me? She has already read To Kill a Mockingbird, Treasure Island, Stargirl, Call of the Wild, Little Women, *and* Hoops. *She is a wiz at history and math, and I can help her with science. I already have a brilliant idea for a science project, but you need four hands to do it. I only have two, of course.*

Twee also likes boys already, so she is way ahead of the game there. She will remind me to wear lip gloss and won't let me dress out of the dirty clothes hamper. I guarantee you I will be a much-better-adjusted seventh grader if I have her with me. If we are separated, and I am bored and unhappy, I could end up a juvenile delinquent, and my mom will be so mad. She might even think it's your fault for not challenging me enough in class.

Believe me, you don't want my mom on your case, Mr. Jimenez.

Yours very sincerely,
Macy L. Hollinquest

CHAPTER TWELVE

The glass doors swooshed open and a blast of air conditioning nearly knocked me over as I stepped into the Los Robles VA Medical Center. A swarm of people in white coats hurried by me with smartphones stuck to the sides of their heads.

I noticed the cops before they noticed me. A couple of them sat behind the information booth, and another one scanned people's stuff with one of those X-ray machines, like they have at the airport. They were big cops and didn't look as friendly as Officer Marley. These guys had big, bulgy muscles and tight pants. I scootched up next to a guy with crutches trying to balance a cup of coffee.

"Here, I can carry that for you," I said. I gave him my most winning smile.

* * * * *

"Thanks," he said with a smile missing most all its teeth. We cruised by the cops in the information booth, and the X-ray cops who were busy checking people through some secure area.

I helped my guy get settled in an oversize chair, then hurried over to a large directory sign and studied it. Looked like they had about a gazillion different departments. I didn't know where to begin. It was mostly hospital stuff, like laboratory, MRI, and radiology. I was all the way down to the S section when my heart leaped into a half gainer. There it was in black and white: "Special Projects: Ninth Floor."

That had to be it! I bolted for the nearest elevator and then chewed down my last fingernail while I read the big sign on the wall: "An adult must accompany all children under the age of 14 on floors 2–9."

I did a quick boob check. At my age I hear they can almost grow right before your eyes. I hadn't really looked at them for a few days. I sighed. Nope. My chest was still an elementary-schooler's. No way I'd be passing for fourteen with these puppies. Plus, no fourteen-year-old girl would be caught out in public with clothes as stained and stinky as mine.

I backed away, trying not to attract attention. As I hunted for the stairs, I found myself wishing for one of those Harry Potter invisibility cloaks. It would come in very handy about now.

Nine flights of stairs is way more than it sounds like! I had a good sweat going by the time I got there. I followed the signs for "Reception," which, turns out, should read "Reception and Nosy Guard." He was leaning up against the counter, all eight hundred muscly pounds of him, talking to a girl working on a computer. His eyebrows lifted when he saw me.

"Lose your way, miss?" he asked.

I tried to straighten the front of my shirt, which was stiff with something gross from the Dumpster. "Uh, well, no, not exactly, sir. Not lost, I mean." I hooked my hair behind my ear. "My mom sent me up. We're looking for my dad, and I think he works up here in Special Projects."

"What's your dad's name?" the girl asked.

"Montgomery Hollinquest—but everyone calls him Gum."

She shook her head. "No one by that name on this floor." She looked over at the cop. "DeVaughn, does that name ring any bells for you?"

"Can't say that it does. You sure this is the right floor, young lady?"

I tried to pick my heart up off the ground while I reached for my pack. Pulling out the letter from my dad, I showed him the return address first and then pulled out the letter.

"See? Says here he's working on a special project."

While the cop read through the letter, I scanned it over again. My eyes caught on the last line, which I loved and had memorized. *I see your smile everywhere, even in—*

"Is your dad a patient here?" the girl asked. A little too kindly, I thought.

"Nope, he's not sick or anything. He works here," I explained.

"Hold on a sec, let me check our directory." Her fingers raced over the keyboard.

"And your mom doesn't know what floor to find him on?" the cop asked, eyeing me over and reaching for his walkie-talkie.

I could feel a case of serious cop-itis coming over him quick. His nostrils twitched, like he might be smelling something fishy.

"Uh, yeah, she's looking on the fourth floor. Sometimes my dad works in a lot of different places. We never know when we come exactly what floor he'll be on. But we always find him," I assured him. Hot beads of sweat popped up on my scalp. "Then we all go to the cafeteria together. My dad loves the pizza there! In fact, that's probably where they both are now, so I better go. They're probably wondering where the heck I am." I backed toward the elevator. "Thanks for everything, ma'am, sir!"

I lunged for the elevator, which had mercifully opened, like *presto!* just when I needed it. That almost never happened in real life. It was packed, and I ducked in and wiggled my way to the back. It was like a doctor convention in there, and it smelled like very clean hands. A few docs had turbans on their heads, and all of them had stethoscopes draped around their necks. There were a few nurses I noticed, too. Mostly, they just looked very tired.

I couldn't even reach the elevator buttons, because we were so squished. But it didn't matter because I was fresh out of ideas.

The elevator plunged downward, as if the cable had snapped, and I gasped. Everyone else kept talking, like they hadn't noticed. I turned myself to face a small tight corner. I tried to breathe into that tiny space. It was the worst elevator in the world! It took big swoopy plunges and made fast stops. I seriously was going to call my congressperson, maybe even the president, when this was all over to complain about the elevator at the VA. This thing wasn't an elevator; it was a plungevator!

I thought about getting off, but I was betting

Gorilla Cop would be waiting for me. He probably had all the floors covered with his buddies.

At last the mob exited, freeing up big pockets of air. Secondhand air, but air all the same. I took deep mouthfuls of it. I added elevators to my list of transportation systems I hate. It was stairs for me for the rest of my life. As I neared the front of the elevator at last, another VA cop came into view. His mouth was plastered to his radio, and he was checking the crowd that had just gotten off.

I fell back into the elevator and pressed myself against the side. I stabbed every possible button to make the elevator go *now*. The cop got a visual on me and started moving toward the door.

Ding, ding! The doors slid closed, almost—

A hand shot through the opening, parting them. But not big hairy hands ready to grab me by the neck. A slim hand with light-blue nail polish and three silver bands stacked up a thumb. Then the rest of her stepped in. Thankfully, without a pair of handcuffs, a pistol, or a club. She gave me a nice smile. She pressed the nine button and then looked at me. "Going up?"

She didn't assume I was up to no good, so I loved her immediately. I stole a long glance at her. She had red, woolly hair and a delicate face. Her name badge read "Karen Eckstein" and then a lot of letters after that. Like she had a lot of college degrees. Under that in large letters, it read "Project Evenstar."

As if she felt me staring, she looked over at me. "Not a big fan of elevators, are you?"

I shook my head slowly, wondering how she knew.

"I saw you on the ride down in the corner," she said. "Looked like you were having a tough time. I thought maybe your mom was on the elevator, and she'd get you off and you'd be okay." She paused a moment. "But then everyone got off and you were all alone. You looked like you might need a hand, so I came back for you."

I bit my lip.

"That officer looking for you?"

I let out a big shaky breath.

"Is there anything I can do?" she asked.

I tried to talk, but I'd lost my voice in all the plunging.

"Macy," she said, her voice soft as a pigeon's coo. "Are you here to see your dad?"

My mouth dropped open, like the tailgate of an old Ford truck.

"You look just like him, you know."

My eyes dropped back to her name badge and burned a hole into it.

"Project Evenstar," it read. *I see your smile everywhere, even in the stars.*

My heart started to gallop. "Do you know where my dad is?" I asked, breathless.

"Yes," she said simply. "He's with me."

CHAPTER THIRTEEN

I splashed a bucket's worth of water on my face in the ladies' room and tried to rub some of the stains out of my shirt with a wet paper towel. I hated to have Dad see me looking so awful. Dr. Eckstein came back a few moments later and handed me a soft, gray T-shirt. "I found this in my gym bag. It might be a little big, but you can tie it at the bottom. Want to wear it?"

I nodded, grateful, turned my back a second, and exchanged shirts. I stuffed my dirty one in my pack.

"I just tried to call your mom, but she's not home," she said.

Uh. Oh. I tried to look nonchalant, but the tips of my ears grew hot.

Dr. Eckstein leaned up against the sink. "I just wanted her to know you had arrived safely."

* * * *

"Oh, she never worries when I'm with Twee and her mom. Twee's mom is completely responsible. She's been driving for years."

She just stared at me, her head to one side, like she was waiting for something else.

That was it, I decided. I was going straight to hell someday. In fact, I was probably going to get elected president of hell. I hurried on to fill in the uncomfortable hole that my lie had dug. "Yeah, when I told Mom last night I wanted to come visit Dad before school started, she thought that was a great idea. Twee and her mom were headed here for some shopping, so it worked out perfect."

"Macy, did you and your mom talk at all about why your dad is here?"

I had a feeling this was leading somewhere, but I couldn't tell where, so I played it supercool.

"Oh, yeah, we had a long talk about it," I improvised. Well, we did have a talk, but not exactly about why he was here. It was more about why he wasn't at home, but that was a minor detail.

"So, how are you feeling about all this?" Her eyes were intent on my face.

Boy, I knew there were some right answers and wrong answers here, but which was which? "Well, I miss him a lot, but I know Project Evenstar is very important. If it wasn't, he'd be home with us."

She gave me a half smile, and I could tell I'd hit on a right answer.

"Well, then, let's head on over, shall we?" she asked, putting out her hand.

We left the big hospital building via the stairs, and Dr. Eckstein led me across a grassy park, surrounded by picnic tables, a horseshoe pit, and an old barbecue. We walked into a long, cool brick building disguised in ivy.

She parked me in a plain-looking lobby, with a few chairs, some bad magazines, and golden oldies being piped in overhead. "Macy," she said, squatting next to me. "I need you to wait here for just a few minutes. I need to check and see if your dad is as ready to see you as you are to see him."

I drew my eyebrows together, confused. "What—" I started.

She hurried to explain. "He's been missing you something fierce. I just want to be sure today is the right time for both of you. This is very important, this first visit."

I tried to sit back in the chair after she left, but I was too nervous. I couldn't quite explain it. This whole Project Evenstar was a mystery, and kind of a spooky one at that. Had they run freaky scientific experiments on my dad here? Changed his appearance, so he could run some black ops? Dr. Eckstein was definitely trying to prepare me for something. That much, I could tell. But what, I had no idea.

The minutes ticked by in slow motion. All the magazines were about two years old. They had a battered copy of *Highlights* magazine, but I stopped reading those years ago. I spotted a bulletin board on the wall across from me. It had the same prayer tacked up that Nana had stuck to the side of her cash register for as long as I could remember.

Lord, grant me the serenity to accept the things I cannot change,
the courage to change the things that I can,
and the wisdom to know the difference.

I asked her about it once. She said it kept her sane.

There were some photographs under that, and I went over to look at them. Looked like a Ping-Pong tournament, with a bunch of guys cutting up about it. Didn't see my dad in any of the pictures, though. Next to that was an index card someone had written, looking to share a ride to Los Robles on visiting day. Then a big long schedule of AA meetings. Was AA the car-towing place? I never could remember. Either way, you could pretty much find an AA meeting about any time of the day around here.

The lobby door opened, and a high school kid came in, with an attitude you could smell for miles. He looked like someone on my mom's caseload. He jutted his chin in my direction and sat down. Hung an unlit cigarette on his lip. After he cracked each of his knuckles and neck in each possible direction, he asked, "How come you're here today? You get a special visiting pass, too?"

"Um, yeah. Dr. Eckstein brought me over. I'm just here to visit my dad. He works here on the project," I explained.

"Is he one of the docs?" he asked.

"No, he's not a doctor. He was in the army. But now he's been assigned to Project Evenstar."

The kid took an imaginary hit off his unlit cigarette. "Yeah, well, my old man has been 'assigned' here three times, and he never stays. He's got seven days in rehab this time, and I *ain't* holding my breath." He stabbed a dirty finger in my direction.

The word "rehab" came at me like a rogue wave. I caught my breath and sailed over the top of it. "I'm, um, sorry— Uh, wull, I hope he makes it. I mean, does better making it . . . this time."

"Is your dad getting out today? Is that why you're

here? 'Cos usually they only let families call or visit on Saturdays."

"No," I said, my windpipe getting narrower by the second. "He's not getting *out*— I mean he doesn't come here for that. He's not in for— He doesn't need rehab. He's working on a secret project for the government."

My words hung there, in the air, for just a second. My heart twisted as I heard, suddenly, how stupid they sounded.

For one nanosecond, the kid flashed me a soft look, like he understood. But then a big, sarcastic smile took over his face. "That's a good one! Yeah, my old man's working on the secret project too. His code name is Agent Alvarez. What's your dad's secret name?"

I heard footsteps coming down the hall. Every step closer made my heart thump harder.

"Macy? You ready? Come on back." Dr. Eckstein waved to me from the door. She spied the kid next to me. "Hey, Thomas. How are you doing today?"

He grunted and looked away.

My legs felt paralyzed under me. I willed them to get me up and walk me toward her. Right, left, right, left. Every step I took felt dangerous. Like if I wasn't very careful, my entire world might explode. I moved into the hallway with her.

She closed the door to the waiting room and

looked down at me. "Okay?"

I swallowed. "Does my dad, uh, *work* here?" I whispered. It all felt, suddenly, like some kind of bad dream.

She nodded. "Work is a very important part of the treatment. Your dad is assigned to the kitchen some evenings, and works in the garden, too."

I licked my lips. Part of my brain tried to make sense of what I was hearing. The other part was trying desperately not to understand.

"Macy?" A figure stepped out of one of the rooms down the hall. The person was wearing sweats and an old T-shirt and was pretending to be my dad. He held on to the doorframe and looked at me. I took a few steps toward him. Dr. Eckstein had her hand on the small of my back, guiding me.

But it wasn't my dad, after all. No, I decided, it couldn't be.

My dad wasn't that skinny, and my dad didn't ever forget to shave. My dad didn't work in anybody's kitchen, and my dad didn't live in a redbrick building in a hospital. My dad didn't have messy hair in the middle of the day and clothes that hung on him and that empty, hollowed-out look in his eyes.

And *my dad definitely, 100 percent for sure didn't need any stupid damn rehab.*

Hot tears burned at the corners of my eyes. I jumped back before the land mine blew up in my face. I threw myself at the waiting-room door—almost pulled it right off its hinges.

I ran like my whole life was on fire, and I had to get away—or be eaten alive by it.

It was seven o'clock straight up at Boomtown Sounds, and no Switch in sight. I checked for messages so many times that the pink-haired girl behind the counter swore she'd personally come find me if he called. I couldn't sit; I couldn't stand. I could barely stand to be in my skin. And, mostly, I couldn't bear to be in my brain.

I didn't want to think about what had just happened. I *couldn't* think about it. But it was like a computer virus was trying to hack the inside of my mind. I knew if I didn't fight it, the virus would change everything I knew and everyone I trusted. It was *wrong, wrong, wrong*, and I would not let it in.

I walked in spirals through the store, starting with the perimeter, then one row in, then another, until I was one small spiral all alone in the middle. Then I'd start over again.

C'mon, Switch!

At fifteen past seven, I went to the pay phone

out front to call Twee. Pink Hair wouldn't let me make a long-distance call on the store's phone. Mrs. Melting Pot said Twee wasn't home. Said she was still babysitting over at my house. That didn't sound right to me, but I wasn't about to blow her alibi if that was what it was. My mom should be home by now.

I went and sat down on the curb out front. I couldn't take any more of Boomtown for a while. The music was so loud, I couldn't think. It was still plenty light outside. The sidewalk was warm under my shorts, and I wished I were sitting in front of Nana's with Twee.

I liked to think that as far as our friendship went, *I* was the brave one, the strong one. But the truth was, there wasn't anybody much stronger than Twee. Even though her adopted family was mostly pretty cool and they really loved her, I knew it was still hard for her sometimes. She had to live with so many questions that she couldn't answer. She had to live with the fact that her own mother had given her away—and she probably would never know why. Despite that, Twee was grateful for what she had, not what she lost. I fought and scrapped for everything I lost. Wouldn't give up anything without a good fight. Except for today.

I'd run right out on my dad. But that skinny guy in rehab wasn't the dad I'd come to get.

Now, I was really glad I hadn't brought Twee with me. What would she think if she knew he was in a place like that? It would have killed me to have her see Dad nearly locked up like some kind of criminal. Like some kind of addict.

Was that why he couldn't come home for my birthday? What was he *doing* there?

I reached into my pack and pulled out a swaybacked Chunky bar. Ripped the end off and took an enormous bite. I tried to chew it, but it tasted like a stick. Nothing was right today. Nothing was the way it was supposed to be. I felt like I'd woken up in the wrong country to the wrong family. I wanted to get back in my old life. I wanted to lie on the floor with my baby brother and watch cartoons.

I swiped an angry tear away with my forearm. I had to think this through. I was over a hundred miles from home. I only had eleven dollars on me. I couldn't risk calling my house to talk to Twee, in case my mom was there with her. I had no idea what had happened to Switch. He could be buzzing his way merrily home, or he could be sitting in the slammer charged with grand theft auto—or grand theft motorcycle, I guess.

If Twee were here, I know she'd tell me to call my mom. But if I did, she'd come get me, and I'd be forced to ride home in the car with her. Trapped with her for a couple of hours. Forced to hear stuff I didn't want to hear. Stuff that might just make my head explode. Stuff that wasn't true. Couldn't be true.

I rubbed Mr. McDougall's collar that I still wore around my wrist. I looked at Ginger's phone number on the metal tag. I could call her. At least I'd be able to find out if she'd reported her bike stolen. Then maybe I'd know if Switch was in big trouble.

"Can I buy you an iced double latte?" A large figure loomed, then squatted next to me.

"Chuck?" I gasped, my voice full of surprise. "What are you doing here?" I wanted to sound irritated, even though I would have been glad to see anyone I knew right then. But I didn't want *him* to know that.

"Switch called me. He asked me to come meet you here."

"Switch? Is he with you?" I jumped up, excited, my head doing a quick 360-degree revolution.

"'Fraid not. He's kind of tied up right now."

Dread reared up, and I closed my eyes a second. "Did he get arrested?"

"Yup."

"But he's okay, right?"

"Well, he's safe. How about you, though? Are you all right? From what I heard of it, you've had quite a day."

I wet my lips, studied my shoes. "M'okay." Liar.

"Can I give you a lift home? Or did you already call your mom? Is she on her way?"

I shrugged my shoulders and shivered. There was a hot summer wind blowing, but I was chilled to my core.

He went on. "After Switch called me, I tried to get your mom on the phone, but she didn't pick up. I've left messages."

I looked up at him. "You drove all this way to come get me?"

"That's part of it," he said. "But I also wanted to check on Switch over in juvenile hall. He's refusing to go back to his foster parents. Again." Chuck shook his head. "Did you know that he was a runaway? Apparently, he's been sleeping all week at the bus station."

I remembered the brown bag I'd seen him with on the bus. I'd figured it was just food or something, but it must have been his whole life in a sack.

Chuck raked his fingers through his hair. "After they picked him up at the drive-in, the cops called Ginger. She verified he hadn't stolen the bike. But when she heard that the two of you had ridden it all the way to Los Robles, she was very concerned. She just thought he was riding it around the neighborhood looking for her dog."

"So if she said he didn't steal it, they'll let him go, right? Can we go get him?"

"No, the judge won't release him unless he goes back to his foster parents or until another foster placement can be located."

"Sounds like Switch has been through them all already," I said.

"I know," Chuck said. "So, if you don't mind, I'm going over there now to check on him. Then I'll take you home."

"Okay," I said.

"One condition, though," he said. "You're calling your mother every five minutes until we reach her. Got it? I've got my cell in the van," he said, motioning behind him.

I nodded in quiet agreement. I'd agree to anything at this point to avoid becoming a permanent resident of Boomtown. I followed Chuck's long strides down the sidewalk.

"Have you eaten anything since lunch?" he asked.

"No, but I'm not hungry," I said. I was actually famished and could have eaten the jeep we'd just passed, but I wouldn't let him know it. He could take me home, but that's where I drew the line.

"S'too bad," he said, fumbling for his keys. "I brought you and Switch some takeout. Thought we could all have a bite over there together. Might be his last decent meal for a while." He unlocked the passenger door and opened it for me.

But I stood staring at the side of his van; gaping, really.

Gaping at the drawing of Buster's "little lima beans" all over the side panel of Chuck's van, which weren't lima beans at all—but big, brown coffee beans, tumbling all over the "fancy and loopy" writing that spelled . . .

"Caffeine Nana's."

After the day I'd had, it made only perfect sense that I was about to climb into the getaway van with Mr. McDougall's kidnapper.

CHAPTER FOURTEEN

I climbed into the front seat holding my breath, like any second I might trigger the Pesky Kid Trap and a giant net would fall over my head. I chanced a quick look over my shoulder in the event that Mr. McDougall was sitting in back, bound and gagged and, hopefully, tail still wagging.

No such luck. The back was filled with about a dozen giant burlap sacks of coffee. At least I hoped they were sacks of coffee! Maybe Caffeine Nana's was just a front for his real business—stealing pets from old ladies for ransom! Even worse, maybe he sold the animals to those research hospitals that liked to test makeup and new drugs. Twee said she saw a special about it on TV. They'd put, like, eighty coats of mascara on a cat's whiskers to see what would

*　*　*　*

happen. Or they'd splash perfume in a rat's eyes to see if it made it go blind. If not, bottle it up and send it out for sale.

There was a large picnic basket right behind my seat that was putting out some potent kid-seducing aromas. I smelled barbecue ribs—one of my major weaknesses. I loved ribs so much I could probably eat them raw. Did Chuck know? How? There was only one answer. It wasn't enough that he took Nana's restaurant from our family. Now, he was working on getting *Mom*.

But what he didn't know was that I was on to him. He didn't know that I now knew he was a *dognapper*.

Oh, he was lower than low. He was subterranean despicable. A hairy, infected wart on a tick's butt!

My head was swimming with rage, hunger, and exhaustion. And the smell of those ribs was making me crazy. I think they had been marinated in Cajun sauce, which I totally adore.

Chuck reached into the center console between our seats and popped it open. I caught my breath as he pulled out a small, dark 45-caliber snub-nosed—

Cell phone.

"Call your mom."

I tried to will my heart still with my mind. Chuck was busy maneuvering into traffic, so I stole a quick look at the numbers he'd recently called. Wanted to see if he'd really been trying to call my mom. That's when I noticed the number that belonged to this phone. It was a number I'd just studied less than five minutes ago: (555) 555-0190.

It was Ginger's number! Weakened with hunger, I blurted before I could stop myself. "This is Ginger's phone! What are you doing with her phone?"

Chuck glanced over at me, puzzled. "That's not Ginger's phone, it's mine."

I ripped Mr. McDougall's collar off my wrist and jangled it near him, like a prosecutor with the smoking gun. "Oh, *yeah*? Then why is it the same number that is on Mr. McDougall's collar?" I thrust it under his nose.

He took it from my hand, looked at it, and then tried to swallow his rather large Adam's apple. He exhaled and laid the collar across his thigh. Rubbed his thumb across the tag. "Where'd you find this?"

"It was in the sidecar of Ginger's bike, under the pillow," I said, still triumphant. "So, tell me, Mr. I'm Such a Nice Guy, how do you explain *that*?"

"Mr. McDougall was my dog," he said. "Mine and Phillip's."

"Who the *heck* is Phillip?" I yelled.

Chuck looked over at me, gauging me a bit.

192

"Phillip," he said, his voice straining over the name, "was my life partner." He flicked on the headlights in the dusk. "And Ginger's son."

Silence struck me, and I circled over all this shiny new information, like a crow trying to decide which piece to pick up.

I kept trying to pass over the "was" in "was my life partner." I tried to ignore the deep sadness that was suddenly thick as fog inside the van. But I couldn't.

I knew sad. It had taken up residence in me the day Nana died. And I knew when it was real. Like I knew Ginger's sadness the day I first met her. And now, was I getting to know . . . Chuck's?

"He's dead," Chuck said, answering the question I didn't want to ask. He stopped for a red light and then looked out the window, away from me. "Phillip died about three years ago."

I knew what "life partner" meant. Mom explained it to me a while back. I knew it meant two people who were the same sex who loved each other enough to get married.

"I'm sorry," I said in a small, confused voice.

He picked up Mr. McDougall's collar and studied it a second. "Phillip and I adopted Mr. McDougall from the shelter when he was just a pup. He was our baby. We were crazy about him."

"Why'd you name him Mr. McDougall?" I asked dumbly, because I didn't know what else to say.

He smiled with one corner of his mouth. "It was just a funny name Phillip and I used to call each other when one of us would do something goofy or clumsy. The first day we had our puppy, everything he did was a 'McDougall.' He kept stepping right smack into his food and water bowls, or he would run up to them and send them flying across the room. It seemed a perfect name for him."

"So how come Ginger had him, then?" I asked.

"After Phillip died," he said, and I knew that had to be the hardest string of words in his vocabulary, "Ginger went to pieces. She and I both did, but he was her only son, her beautiful Phillip. She'd been a single mother, so he was all she had. I wanted to do something, give her something, anything, to make the hurt less."

He stopped a moment, and I wondered if he'd continue. After a pause, he did. "So, I gave her Mr. McDougall, who Phillip adored." Chuck blew out a deep, shaky breath. "I told her I was going to be too busy with the café to take care of him anymore. Which wasn't true, but it was the only way she would have taken him from me."

"But wasn't that hard?" I asked, afraid of the answer.

He looked over at me, his face full of grief. He nodded. "It almost killed me," he said, and his voice cracked. "It was like losing Phillip twice."

I thought about how that must have been for Ginger—losing her son and then having his dog come up missing. Losing them both, she must have been—

"Ohhh," I said, breathless, as pieces fell softly together. The food, the clean hair-free furniture, that neighbor boy's story of Mr. McDougall being "kidnapped."

"Mr. McDougall died at Ginger's house, didn't he?"

Chuck nodded his head slowly.

"And you," I said, my voice halting. "She called *you*, and you went to get him so you could bury him." I pressed my lips together hard. I had to keep asking until I could make it real. "Was Ginger *there* when Mr. McDougall died?"

"Yes."

"But she won't remember it, will she?"

Chuck wiped his eyes on the collar of his shirt. "I think she can't. She can't take any more. It's just too much."

I nodded, knowing. Knowing that place she had found to go when things just got so hard. In that place, you just stopped seeing. Even the things that were right in front of you.

Like with Dad. There was something Mom knew. Something Twee saw. Something wrong with him I never wanted to face. And so, I guess, I just didn't see it.

I hung my head. Tears ran a course down my face then, leaving a big wet spot on my shirt, right over the place of my heart.

CHAPTER FIFTEEN

The scariest thing about county juvenile hall wasn't the sound of the heavy metal doors that clanked behind us or even the three burly boys in orange jumpsuits mopping the floor. It was the look my mother gave me when she came to fetch Chuck and me from the guard's station. It was combustible. That look could launch rockets out of NASA. And after the day I'd just had, you'd think nothing would surprise me. But having Mom come out of the locked-up side of juvie with her eyes lasered on me was like a knee to the solar plexus.

I tried to swallow. "Hi, Mom," I squeaked, mouse-like.

She crossed her arms over her chest.

We waited while a uniformed officer with a tree

trunk for a neck searched through Chuck's picnic basket for contraband. He took out the plastic knives and forks and then dropped them into a bin below his desk. Just in case Chuck and I decided to help Switch dig his way out of the joint with a white plastic knife, I guessed.

"Okay, clear," the guard said, giving my mom a nod.

"Follow me" was all she said.

We took up behind her down a long hallway with a very shiny floor. Chuck gave my shoulder a quick squeeze, and I prepared myself for the biggest mess of trouble I had ever cooked up in my life.

Mom pressed her badge into a metal plate next to a door that read "Mediation." It clicked open, and she held the door as Chuck and I passed through into a room with a giant, long table. Occupied by one buzz-headed kid.

"Switch!" I started to head over to him, except that Mom reeled me in by the back of my shirt. "No sir, young lady. No sir."

"Oh man, Macy, I'm glad you're okay!" Then he looked over at Chuck. "Thanks for picking her up and everything." He took a long deep breath and then dropped his head between his hands for a minute.

Mom pulled me by the shoulders, swinging me around until I was facing her. She squeezed me hard against her and then whispered for my ears only. "I have never been so scared or so glad to see anyone in my entire life." Her voice wobbled at the end, and she cleared her throat hard.

"I'm sorry, Mom. I—"

"*Later.* We're going to sort all this out. Okay?" She gave me a little shake and then buried her face in my hair for a second.

I nodded, and she straightened herself up.

"You two could be sisters," Switch said. "I would have never guessed mother and daughter."

"Can it, Terrance," Mom said. She put her hands on her hips and blew out a breath. "I hardly know where to begin with you two."

"How about with dinner?" Chuck asked. "These kids need to eat, Elise. It's been a very long day."

She nodded and squeezed the bridge of her nose while Chuck set out paper plates and opened boxes of baby back ribs, steak fries, and barbecued beans. And an entire half slab of chocolate cake. Switch and I leaped at the food, like a couple of wolverines.

While Chuck and Mom talked together in hushed voices at the back of the room, Switch whispered over a rib. "Would it have killed you to let me know your mom was a probation officer? And mine in particular?"

I shoved a load of beans into my mouth and

shrugged. "Guess before you take a girl off on a crime spree, you should at least find out her last name."

Switch looked at me across the table with that nervous kind of look someone gets when you've made a horrendous mess on your face. They're hoping you'll catch on soon before they have to tell you.

I mopped my mouth with a napkin, which came away bright red. If you hadn't known it was Cajun barbecue sauce, you might have thought I'd just suffered a gunshot wound to my face.

"Sorry," I said. "I'm starved."

Switch smiled and loaded his spoon with a chunk of chocolate cake. "Hey, any chance I'm going to find a key baked in here?"

"Sorry, I didn't make the cake. I was kinda busy today."

I studied him a moment while he ate. He looked worse than I did. He'd apparently spent a couple of hours in the Dumpster before the cops nabbed him.

"Terrance, Macy?" Mom called. "We're going to step out into the hallway a moment to make a call. Finish your dinners. But I'm standing right here." She tapped on the door's window letting us know she'd have one eye on us the whole time.

"*That's* gotta be tough," Switch said, pointing his chin in Mom's direction.

"I suppose there are worse things."

"So? You still haven't told me about your dad. Did you find him or what?"

I got up and threw my paper plate into the corner wastebasket, under a huge American flag. Wiped a few crumbs from the old polished finish of the long table. Studied a framed copy of the Bill of Rights posted on the wall.

"You going to answer me any time today?" Switch asked, wiping his index finger carefully with his napkin.

I shrugged.

"Okay, guess not."

"What do you think is going to happen to you?" I asked. "I mean, how long could they actually keep you here?"

"They can keep me as long as they want, if they think there's a danger that I'll run away again. Since I'm a ward of the court, they get to call the shots." He polished off the rest of his cake. "I don't care what they say. I'm not going back to the Gilberts' house, and I'm not going back to the Cosgrows, or the Reyburns, or the Thompsons, or the Fagens. And I am absolutely not ever, ever, *ever* going back to the Arnolds," he said, the muscle in his jaw flexed. He clasped his fingers together until his knuckles were white and his fingertips bright red.

I went and sat next to him.

He picked up his plastic spoon and snapped it in two.

I took it away from him.

"I've had it up to here with what people think will be good for me—tough love, outward bound, inward out, sports camp, young farmers, and all the other 'fix the foster kid' programs."

I wanted to pat him somehow, but I didn't know how or where. *Best to just sit,* I thought.

The door clicked open, and he sat back up straighter, feelings quickly erased from his face. Except the one that said, *What do I care what you do with me?*

"I called the judge," Mom said, looking at Switch. "I wanted to talk to her about our options. If you really don't want to go back to the Gilberts—"

"I really *won't*," he said, his voice hard.

"Terrance, I hate to book you. You don't really belong here, but you're making this very difficult. It's my job to keep you safe. Sleeping on the Greyhound bus is not an option." She tapped her pen hard against the table and now looked at us both. "You two are very, very lucky that Ms. Grady is not pressing any theft charges. Terrance, you don't even have a driver's license, and you," she said, shooting me a deadly look, "are grounded until your senior prom."

A protest rose up, but I let it go.

She closed her eyes a moment. "When I think of what could have happened to either of you today—"

"But didn't, Elise. Nothing bad happened," Chuck reminded her. "They're both safe."

"I thought your sudden interest in the Green Angels was a little suspect," she said. "I got the real story, or at least part of the real story, out of Twee first thing this morning. Did you two even go to Raging Falls? Your aunt Liv and I spent half the day there looking for you."

Switch and I looked at each other, realizing we'd forgotten to get our stories straight.

"I think I'd like to take the Fifth," I said.

CHAPTER SIXTEEN

66 Me too," Switch chimed in. "I take the Fifth."

"Denied," Mom said. She tapped her pen on the thick case file in front of her. "Then I get a call that one of my runaways has been picked up in Los Robles and is raising bloody Cain with the cops. He's yelling about a girl named Macy who is stranded at Boomtown Records."

I had to smile. Switch had been worried about me. How about that?

"Ah," Chuck said.

"Yes, ah," Mom said. "I was on my way downtown to rescue this mysterious stranded girl named Macy, but Terrance told me *you* were on your way."

I could tell we were going to have a long, hard

* * * * *

talk on the way home about what I'd really been up to all day.

Switch cleared his throat and shredded a nearby napkin, like a nervous chipmunk. "If I refuse to go into any more foster homes, will they just keep me locked up till I'm eighteen? I'd just as soon be here than with some messed-up foster family. Really, I don't mind. The food's decent. The staff is pretty nice if you stick to their rules. I can live with that."

Mom closed the files in front of her and then looked at her watch. "We'll revisit that tomorrow, Terrance. This has been quite a day."

"Does Dana still work here?" Switch asked. He turned to me. "I've done time here before, and Dana is a really cool counselor. She tells some seriously grizzly ghost stories at night." He glanced quickly at my mom. "I mean, *after* we finish our team-building circle and trust falls at night."

"Mmm-hmm," Mom said, "I'll bet."

She gave him a small smile, and I could see that underneath all the mad, she really liked Switch. "Yep, Dana's here. She was asking about you. I'll call her to come process you and take you back to your bunk."

Next, she looked over at me. "One of us needs to call Twee. She's been worried sick about you all day."

I jumped out of my seat, like a rocket launched. "I'll call her, please?"

She handed me her cell phone and a stern look. "Three minutes. Just the facts. Oh, and tell her we'll be home around eleven. She should put Jack to bed now, if she hasn't already. I called her mom and cleared it with her so that Twee could stay late."

I went into the hall and ducked into the girls' restroom for some privacy. Then I dialed the number. "Twee! It's me!" I said when she picked up, her voice breathless.

"MACY! Where have you been? Everybody's looking— Oh man, you are in such trouble with your mother!"

"I know—"

"I told her!! I am so-so-so sorry! But she used that probation officer thing on me, and I just caved. She said something about me being an 'accessory after the fact'—"

"Twee, its *okay*! I'm with my mom. We're coming home. She said to put Jack to bed."

"What happened?" she yelled into the phone.

An older girl with a lot of tattoos and very stiff hair came into the restroom. I turned away and covered my mouth, so she couldn't hear me. "Twee," I blurted in a rush. "Look, I lied about today. And I'm sorry. I hated lying to you."

"You didn't go with Switch after all?" she asked, sounding relieved. "Where the heck have you been all day?"

"Well, I did go with Switch, but not to Raging Falls. I had him take me to Los Robles."

I could hear her suck in her breath, even all these miles away. "Did you find him?" she asked breathlessly.

I buried my teeth in my thumbnail. "No," I said. I looked up in the bathroom mirror, took my thumb away from my mouth. "Least not— Well, no . . . he wasn't really there."

Which was true. The dad I knew, my personal superhero, my life coconspirator—he was gone. What was left in his place was not anyone I recognized.

In the end Chuck convinced my mom to leave her government car at juvenile hall, and he drove the two of us home. Said he'd feel better if she just took it easy for a while.

Mom looked like she might argue with him, but then just went along. Maybe she wasn't looking forward to being alone with me, either.

Chuck was, it turned out, pretty thoughtful. Maybe he'd always been, but when you're looking for someone to be a giant creep no matter what, it's hard to notice when they do something uncreepy.

And he wasn't trying to get my mom to fall in love with him. Chuck had a broken heart. He was just trying to get by. Like I was. Like Ginger was.

My mom sat in the front seat of Chuck's car and pulled her big clip out of her hair. That was her sign for going off duty. Then she reached behind the seat, searching for my hand.

I gave it to her, and we just both held on for a while.

Chuck put on some soft music, and they talked a long time about Switch. About how a kid like him could end up so much worse if he didn't get a real chance at a stable home. But my ears were too tired to pay attention. I fell asleep—almost a coma, really—and slept a very long time.

Dear Mr. Jimenez,

The Sixth Thing About Me: this one is sort of secret, so please don't tell anyone. I'll be on the soccer team at Kit Carson (that's not the secret), but I really don't want to play soccer. I don't even like it! I love basketball best, and the Kit Carson Cougars could really use me. I watched some of the games last year, and your team is pretty awful. My dad wants me to play soccer, though. It's his favorite sport. I don't want to hurt his feelings. If you have kids, make sure you find out what they like to play best. And even if your kids are better than you at a sport, you should be encouraging and help them play the sport they like.

Yours very sincerely,

Macy L. Hollinquest

PS Last year I also missed learning about Roman numerals during that week I was sick. If I ever go to Italy, I will be in big trouble trying to tell time and paying for pizza.

CHAPTER SEVENTEEN

I ran my hand lightly over the new big window outside Nana's coffee shop. Chuck hadn't had time yet to have a new sign painter come. The glass was still blank.

Caffeine Nana's wasn't open yet. It was still early. Mom had given me permission to leave the house for just one important errand. Then I had to come straight back home. I could see Chuck sitting in one of the booths, working on some papers. He was sitting at my favorite booth—the one that got the best morning sun. He saw me and waved, and then came to the door and unlocked it. He gave me a big smile.

"Can I ask you something—" I started.

"Hey, can I ask you a favor—" His words ran over mine.

We laughed, kinda nervous, both standing in

* * * *

this new place together—the one where we talk like regular people and I am not giving him the stink eye.

"You go," he said.

"Can I, um, come in?" I asked.

He didn't make a big deal about it like he could have. Didn't mention that I'd never been in since he'd bought the place. He just stepped aside and said softly, "Of course."

I breathed in the air that was so familiar. I could almost smell Nana's perfume mixed in with the grill and the leather booths. This early in the day, it was so quiet inside, so cool, with the overhead fan humming its rhythm. I felt almost like I was walking into a holy kind of place—like I was in the presence of what Father Dan at Aunt Liv's church called "things unseen." And they were good things.

So much of me lived in this space, so much of Nana, I thought. It was still hers, and nothing Chuck could do would ever change that. Besides, he wasn't the one who had taken my nana.

I turned and looked back at him. "It looks good in here."

"It does now," he said, with a nice smile. I never had noticed how handsome he was before, really. I went over and perched on one of the old stools. Gave myself a slow spin while I collected my thoughts.

Chuck sank down into a booth and waited.

"I want to go see Ginger this morning," I said. "I'd like to apologize and stuff."

He looked at me, a question in his eyes.

"You know, for giving her a worry about me and Switch. And—and—" I stammered. "And a part of me wants to try to talk to her about Mr. McDougall. But I'm not sure. I just hate for her to keep driving those flyers around and waiting and waiting for him to come home."

"I know," he said. "Well, whatever you decide, I'm sure she'd be glad to see you, Macy. She's grown very fond of you and Twee."

"I'm fond of her, too," I said, realizing just then how very true that was. I paused and then asked, "Would you go with me to see her, Chuck?"

He looked surprised but went right past that. "Sure! I can drive us over, as soon as the morning shift gets here. While we're waiting, will you help me with something?" He pointed to the pile of papers on the table.

I walked over and looked. It was a bunch of sketches of the front window's glass.

"I'm getting these ready for the painter," he explained. "I want it to look just like it did before. Can you help?"

I leaned down on my elbows and studied it.

He went on. "I've got most of it here," he mumbled, "but I don't think it's right. How'd it go? 'Good coffee, good times, good God—'"

I picked up the pencil and crossed out "God." "It's 'good *Lord*,' Chuck, not 'good God.' Nana was very particular about not using God's formal name here."

"Right, right. Got it. Okay, it's 'Good coffee, good times, good Lord'—" He paused and rubbed his forehead, his pencil stuck on its point.

I wrote it out for him and then stared at it. Wondered how I'd missed it for so long. It had been staring at me all those Saturdays I'd been camped out front. A shiver ran straight up my tailbone to my neck. It felt like those "things unseen" were standing very close.

"'Come on in,'" I read, my voice a whisper.

They were my nana's words. I wished I had been listening to them all along.

CHAPTER EIGHTEEN

The sound of a shrieking alarm met us as we pulled into Ginger's driveway. I quickly reached for the door handle, ready to launch.

"Stay here!" Chuck ordered me as he quickly shut off the car and raced toward the front door.

I hurried after him, but he didn't notice. I could smell the smoke coming from Ginger's house, even from the front yard. Chuck grabbed the front doorknob and shoved himself in. The sound of the alarm—maybe even more than one—was earsplitting.

"GINGER!" Chuck yelled as he ran toward the kitchen. The smoke seemed thickest in there. I ran in after him, but I could see she wasn't in there. Smoke was streaming from the oven door and even coming up from under the burners. Chuck grabbed a dish

* * * *

towel to cover his mouth and nose and then tried to turn the oven off. He drew his hand back quickly and cursed. He took the towel from his face and wrapped it around his hand and tried again to turn it off.

He saw me then, and yelled, "OUT! Now!"

But I had to find Ginger. I raced through the rest of the house looking for her. She wasn't in the bedroom or bathroom and study. I ran to the backyard and then doubled back when I remembered her darkroom. She wasn't there, either. She wasn't anywhere to be found.

I hurried back toward the kitchen and found Chuck standing on the counter, trying to turn off the smoke alarm. He had all the doors propped open now, and the smoke was being sucked into a fan over the stove.

There was a very charred-looking cake pan sitting out with a half-burned dish towel next to it.

"SHE'S NOT HERE ANYWHERE!" I shouted over the shrill din.

Chuck gave the alarm a final yank, and the sound shut off. We both groaned in relief as the world went quiet. He eased himself back down and leaned up against the cupboard. He wiped his forehead with the back of his hand.

"What happened?" I asked.

"I'm not sure," he sighed, shaking his head. "Looks

like she left a dish towel in the oven with whatever she was cooking. It caught on fire."

I looked around the kitchen then, and noticed what a mess it was. The last time I had been here it had been spotless. Today, it looked like raccoons had come over and made breakfast. There were dirty dishes out everywhere and a couple of broken eggs on the floor. The refrigerator door was open. I moved toward it slowly and closed it, stepping around the egg mess.

"She's having an off day," Chuck said, surveying the mess with me. "I'm just glad we got here when we did. Did you check the darkroom for her?"

"I looked everywhere. Promise. She's not here."

"She probably went out for a walk. She did that one day a few months ago, after she'd started running water for a bath. By the time she'd gotten back, the place was flooded. Her next-door neighbor called me when he saw the water coming out the front door. He must be out today, or he would have come over when the smoke alarm went off."

"She doesn't seem like someone who would do stuff like this."

"I know. On her good days she could probably run the Senate. But then, some days she isn't fully with us. She gets confused and loses track of what she's doing. She was having one of those kind of days when Mr. McDougall died. I think that's part of why she can't seem to understand that he is really gone."

"Maybe she shouldn't be living by herself. She could have burned the house down!"

He sighed and rubbed the top of his head. "Well, probably would have just smoked the place out pretty bad. But I do worry when she is having one of her bad days what might happen. I've talked to her about selling this place and moving in with me. Or even moving into some kind of active retirement community where she could have some level of supervision. But she won't hear of it. She is as stubborn as Phillip was. That man could have driven the pope to drink."

"Hellooo? Who's there?"

We both turned to see Ginger enter the house. She came into the kitchen looking confused. She glanced from me to Chuck, then from Chuck to me. "Oh dear, was something burning?" She headed toward the stove. "Have you two been cooking?"

"We came by, and your smoke alarm was going off," I blurted. "That's why we barged in."

"That dang thing is always going off," she said. "I'm going to have it removed!"

She looked over at the counter. "Were you two baking a cake? You've burned the tar out of it." She reached for it, and Chuck grabbed her hands.

"It's very hot!" he said. "Let it cool down."

She looked at the charred dish towel on the counter, and Chuck followed her gaze.

"Ginger," he said softly and gently. "You were making a cake earlier—"

"Nooo," she said, shaking her head. "I was out walking."

"Right, but before you went for a walk, you were making a cake, and when you put it in the oven, you seem to have left a dish towel in the oven too."

She put her fingers on her lips. Her whole hand was trembling.

"It's okay, Ginger," I said, putting my arm around her waist. "When my brother was first born, my mom once put a dirty diaper in the fridge instead of the trash."

She looked at me then like she was surprised to see me. "Macy! Would you like some sweet tea? It is hotter than blazes out there."

"Why don't you let me get it?" Chuck said. "You two go sit down, and I'll bring it to you. Macy wanted to have a chat with you, anyway."

"Oh! Well, that would be lovely. Let's do go sit in the living room. I'm beat out from this weather."

"Uh, if you're tired, I could talk to you another

time," I said. I wasn't sure she would understand what I had to say about Mr. McDougall. She hadn't even remembered she was baking a cake.

"Nonsense," she said. "You're the nicest thing that has happened to me all day. I can nap any time."

Once the three of us were settled in her living room behind ice-cold glasses of tea, I couldn't find a place to start. I'd woken up that morning almost desperate to talk to her—to show her what was right in front of her. But now I felt like I was looking out over some kind of ledge. If I started talking, would I fall?

I was perched on the edge of a chair across from Ginger and Chuck, who were sitting on her big couch. They both looked at me as if I might be delivering the Gettysburg Address.

"I—I, well, I wanted to tell you I am really sorry about your motorcycle."

She looked at me blankly.

Oh, geez, had she forgotten that, too? I looked to Chuck for help. I didn't know if I should continue.

Chuck nodded encouragement and then put his hand on Ginger's knee. "Switch took your bike and drove Macy to Los Robles."

"Oh, of course!" she said. "It was very gallant of you kids to try to find Mr. McDougall. Though I'm sure you've given your mother a whole head of gray hair over this. I had no idea you two would expand the search area to Los Robles."

I wiped the palms of my hands on my shorts. The back of my neck was starting to sweat. "We didn't take your bike to go look for Mr. McDougall, Ginger. Switch lied to you about that." And I'd lied to Twee and my mom. It was the biggest day of lies I've ever lived.

She pulled on her ring finger and looked confused. "Oh?"

"Switch took me to Los Robles so I could try to find my dad." Even saying the word "dad" gave my guts a painful twist. I swallowed hard. "He hadn't come home in a long time. I really needed to find him."

"Find him? Macy, is he missing too?" Ginger asked.

I blew out a gusty breath. I think I'd been holding it for a very long time. Months, maybe. "I thought he was." I lifted my shoulders and then let them drop. "But he wasn't missing after all. He just— Well, he just wasn't where I wanted to find him."

Ginger folded her napkin around her iced tea while she sorted through that and then looked up at me. "I didn't realize— I'm sorry. That must be very hard."

Chuck reached over and gave me one of those big-man pats on my knee.

I looked down at my feet. I had on two completely different socks today. How had that happened?

Ginger glanced at Chuck and then back at me. I could tell she was completely lost. But I couldn't stop now that I'd started this.

I clamped my front teeth down on my bottom lip. Hard. The air around me grew thick and close. A trickle of sweat snaked its way down my back.

I hung my head. My nose began to drip. I gave it an embarrassed swipe with my napkin. I squeezed my eyeballs tight a moment, trying to hold off tears. "I'd made up this whole story in my head about why he wasn't coming back home. Turns out I was all wrong."

A hundred pictures flashed through my mind, like a slide show on turbo speed. And in every one, I was the one running around, trying to get everyone together for the perfect family picture. But someone was always missing. Dad was away or Nana was sick or my mom was off mad—or having a baby, or studying, or worrying about money.

"I'm not even used to my nana being dead yet, but if I lose my dad too—" Almost without sound, I said, "It's too much."

I looked up at Ginger and saw that her eyes had begun to water. And I knew in that instant that this was why I wanted to come today. She knew what it meant to go through "too much." And she knew what it was like to swap the truth for a hope that was doomed from the start.

Ginger stiffened back against her chair, took a deep breath. She tried—she did—to keep it all in, but her face crumpled anyway, and she covered her eyes. I felt her giant sadness arrive, like I had when I first met her. It hovered over her.

I looked at Ginger, swiping tears off my face. "Sorry— I just miss— I miss them both so much," I said, my voice heaving.

I went over and knelt down in front of her. I could smell the rich soil from the garden on her clothes.

The two of us just stayed there awhile. I could feel Nana, Phillip, and Mr. McDougall right there with the three of us. There was such aching sweetness in that. That we'd never see them again, never be able to hug them or talk to them—that was the most god-awful hurt.

After a while I reached in my pocket and handed Mr. McDougall's collar to Ginger.

"This was under the pillow of the sidecar."

"Oh!" she said, cupping it in her hand and then

bringing it to her chest. She tried to straighten out her face before she continued. She cleared her throat. "I didn't realize he didn't have his collar on. I suppose that will make it even more difficult for him to be found." She rubbed her thumb over the tag, just as I had when I'd found it.

"Ginger, you—" Chuck started.

"Don't—" she snapped.

"I was just going to say that I'm sorry," he said. "I know how hard all this has been for you."

I gave him a grateful look. Ginger's hope was her life preserver. She deserved to have that for as long as she needed it.

Chuck blew his nose in that funny, noisy way that men do. My dad sounded just like that. I caught my breath until the pain passed.

I handed Ginger a napkin, and she wiped her face. She'd been carrying so much for so long.

A face came to me then: my mother's. I imagined what it must have been like for her to hold all that she had by herself for so many months, maybe years. And then have a daughter who blamed her for most of it.

"Ginger, can I use your phone a minute?" I took a deep, steadying breath. "I need to call home."

CHAPTER NINETEEN

Jack and Mom were out back when I got home, test-driving Jack's new wading pool. When I stuck my head out, he was squealing with all the baby boy gusto he had and splashing most of the pool's water out onto the grass and flower beds.

Mom looked up and smiled at me. "Guess I won't have to water today. Who would have thought a wading pool could become a workingwoman's convenience? I can lounge, entertain my baby, and water my yard!"

Mom rattles on like this when she's nervous. Guess she was worried about the Big Talk we needed to have. I'd left the house early on purpose this morning. I'd been avoiding her big-time.

She motioned back toward the house. "There's some curried chicken sandwiches in the fridge. Grab

* * * * *

one and come on out, Mace."

I went inside and then got my hat and my sunglasses. Covered my nose in zinc. Gee, maybe now she wouldn't even recognize me. As much as it was time for us to talk, I still didn't want to.

I knew we had to. But that didn't change how I felt.

The telephone answering machine light was flashing "2" when I walked by. Since I didn't have a cell phone yet, the old-fashioned answering machine keeps my mom's messages for me while she is working.

The first message was from me, calling from Ginger's to say I'd be home in a little bit. I hated how young I sounded on answering machines. I erased it and then pushed playback again.

Elise, it's Dr. Eckstein again. Just checking to see how you're all doing. Hope Macy is okay. Gum is really worried about her. Will you give me a call back? I'd like to talk about setting up the meeting we discussed last night. Thanks!

I opened the fridge and studied the shelves. I ate a small triangle of sandwich, standing in the fridge's air-conditioned sanctuary. I grabbed a sandwich for Mom, a root beer for me, and headed out.

Jack went crazy when he saw me come back. He slapped his big round baby belly and chortled. He lay down and then kicked his legs furiously underneath him, showing me all his best swimming moves.

"Wow! That's great, Jack!" I said, wishing my sunglasses came with windshield wipers.

Mom and I watched his pretty hilarious antics for a while, until his little teeth started chattering. I hauled him out and then wrapped him up papoose-like in a terry towel. Pulled him on top of me. Like a human shield.

I didn't talk for a while still. Mom was giving me plenty of wide-open space. She'd probably learned this technique in her probation officer training. If you want to get a kid to come out of the bushes, you must be very, very quiet. After a while they'll get so nervous they'll start talking and give themselves away. Normally, I like to blow up her psychological theories about kids, but I was too tired.

"Turns out Mr. McDougall wasn't lost after all," I said.

"No?" she said, putting her magazine down.

"Nope," I said, hugging Jack closer. "He died. Last spring."

Mom turned in her chaise longue to look at me.

I tried to sort it all out as I talked. "I guess Ginger knew that somewhere in her head, but her heart wouldn't let her really know it. So, she kept pretending he was alive if only she could find him." I chewed the end of my thumb. "That doesn't make her crazy, does it?"

Mom popped the top of her sunscreen and then squeezed some into her hand. Leaned over toward me and covered Jack's ears and nose. "Sometimes when we're not ready to hear something painful, we have to keep ourselves very busy not hearing it. It can look crazy, but it's not. It's just coping. We all do that differently."

Jack snorted under the towel. I kissed his wet spiky hair.

"Mom," I asked, my voice almost failing me. "Why did you really sell Nana's to Chuck?"

She pulled her knees up to her chest. I could tell she was measuring out how much she was going to say.

"Mom, just tell me. I'm going to be twelve in two days. I want to hear the whole truth." That last part wasn't so much true. I didn't really want to hear the whole truth, but I knew in my gut I needed to.

She gave me a long look, and I could see myself reflected in her sunglasses. "Before Nana died," she explained, "she put me in charge of all her finances."

"How come you? Why not Dad?" I braced myself for the answer.

Mom was quiet a moment. I knew she was trying

to find just the right words. She took a swig of her bottled water and then went on. "Nana knew Dad had some . . . problems." She looked over at me. "We all knew that, honey."

I looked away.

"And," she continued, "Nana knew Aunt Liv wouldn't be able to handle it, either. Aunt Liv will do anything your dad tells her to do. Neither of them was ready for the responsibility of running the café."

"But when she put you in charge, did she know you were going to sell it?"

Mom nodded. "Nana had been talking to Chuck about buying it before she'd even gotten sick. She knew him from the Chamber of Commerce, and she really liked him, Macy. She was tired and wanted to retire. I think she would have gone ahead and sold it to Chuck then, except your dad convinced her to keep it. He told her he could get out of the service on a medical discharge and run it for her. He promised her that he could handle it."

"But he couldn't?"

"No, and it just broke her heart. We all wanted it to work. But if anything, being out of the service made things worse for your dad. Nana was pretty sick by then, and on top of everything else with him, it was just eating him up. He couldn't cope with losing her."

My mind was busy chewing on the "on top of everything else with him." I thought about the things about my dad that I loved the most. How funny he was, how he loved to do things on the spur of the moment—things that just always seemed to make my mom mad at him. Things that always made Twee get very quiet and kind of bristly around him.

"Aunt Liv and I ended up running the show. Your dad would disappear from work for hours; sometimes he'd be gone overnight. I finally convinced him to go to get some help at the VA. This is his third try. But it's the longest he's ever made it."

"Did Nana know what was going on?"

"She'd always known he had a drinking problem. She said watching Gum was like watching Grandpa all over again." Mom slid down to the end of her chaise and stuck her feet in Jack's little pool.

"A couple of weeks before she died, she asked me to sell the shop to Chuck." She turned and looked back at me. "It was what Nana wanted, Macy."

"But Dad said you were the one—"

"I know what he said. That's part of the crazy thinking that goes with being an alcoholic. Because he can't bear to look at what he has done to us, he has to blame someone else. And in this family, I'm it."

My brain wrestled this idea to the mat. I'd blamed

her for so long that the idea that everything wasn't her fault felt as strange as a foreign language to me. The tricky part was once it stopped being her fault, whose fault was it?

My mind didn't want to go there.

"How long has he been this way?" I asked.

"He's been drinking for as long as I've known him. But it got worse, so much worse, after his first tour in Iraq. Remember when I talked to you about traumatic brain injury?"

I rubbed at the zinc on my nose. "Kind of. You said it was something that happened to the soldiers in Iraq and Afghanistan who had been around a lot of blasts."

"Right, and part of what Project Evenstar does is evaluate injuries to the brain and how they might be affecting someone's behavior. Some of your dad's issues may be related to that. But regardless, he has got to stop drinking. No treatment will help him until he does that."

Things came crashing down on me then, like Nana's front window when Ginger smashed into it. I stood still in all the pieces of broken glass at my feet.

"Why didn't you tell me, Mom? Why didn't you tell me Nana wanted you to sell the shop?"

"I did," she said, putting her hand on my leg. "You just weren't ready to believe it."

I pulled Jack's warm little body closer to me. Laid my face against his head while I tried to sort out my life from the fragments. "You never told me this stuff about Dad."

She turned in her chaise so she was facing me. "I've been composing the conversation in my mind for such a long time." She shook her head. "Your dad begged me not to. He promised he would tell you from the other side—once he got past the addiction. We're just . . . not there yet. Dr. Eckstein is helping me with some of this. About the ways that I've protected your dad over the years by covering for him. I just didn't want him ever to stop being your hero, Macy. A girl needs a hero."

"Are you going to leave him?" I whispered, my voice tight as a violin string.

She gave my hand a squeeze. "We're not there yet, either."

CHAPTER TWENTY

I was upstairs playing a new game with Jack called Hide the Big Sister. It's just like Hide the Baby, but in this version I had to hide and Jack gets to look. Except he'd only look under his little bed for me, so to be nice, I kept hiding behind it. I sure will be glad when his brain grows a little bigger.

Mom was downstairs vacuuming like her life depended on it, with the Dixie Chicks blasting in the background. She asked me to take Jack upstairs for a while so she could get some chores done. We hadn't talked much since the day before, but things felt better between us. Not perfect, but better. She said I was still on house arrest, but I had a feeling she was softening.

After finding his big sister three times in a row,

* * * * *

Jack won a storytime. I dragged him up onto the rocking chair by his bedroom window. He'd picked his very jelly-stained favorite, *Harold and the Purple Crayon.*

I was crazy about that book when I was little. Funny, now it's Jack's favorite. It's a story about a kid who draws all these great adventures with a purple crayon. I always loved that not only could he draw great stories, but when he got in a bind, he could draw himself right out of trouble, too. I used to carry a purple crayon around with me in my pocket, just in case. Sure could have used one this past week. But then, I guess everything worked out okay; just not how I had planned.

I hadn't planned on finding my dad in a rehab center. I hadn't planned that I'd have to look at all the ways he'd made Mom's life so hard the last few years. And I'd helped him in all of that. I'd blamed Mom for ruining everything in our family when all she was trying to do was take care of us. I sure had a lot to sort out. I was lucky to have Twee to help me with that. Mom would be, too.

I kissed Jack's sweaty little forehead. No wonder Mom was so crazy about him. He'd been the only person in our family who didn't blame her for everything.

Jack and I were lost in Harold's adventure when a familiar *rumm-rumm* rumbling came down our street, getting louder by the second.

Jack was mad for anything with a motor. He kicked his legs to get down. I picked him up and carried him to the window.

"Grrrrooom! Grr-grrrr-grrrooom!" he rumbled, spanking the glass.

Chuck, who was riding Ginger's motorcycle, came to a neat stop in our driveway. He turned, smiling to his sidecar passenger. Twee ripped off an enormous pair of riding goggles, and a helmet, and grinned back at him. She didn't tell me she was coming over, and certainly not with *him*. Except he wasn't *him* anymore; he was just him. A pretty decent guy after all.

Then I noticed Aunt Liv's red convertible across the street, parked crookedly, with one wheel up on the sidewalk. And she'd left her trunk open. I shook my head and smiled. At least some things stayed the same in Constant.

I gave Jack a diaper change, and then he rode downstairs on my back, pausing on the landing. I stopped and stared. Mom, Aunt Liv, Chuck, Twee, and *Switch* were all assembled in the living room, each looking very pleased at the confused expression on my face.

"SURPRISE!" they all shouted together, and then threw a load of confetti and streamers at me. It scared the daylights out of poor Jack, who screamed like they were hurling live snakes. He buried his head into me, and his body shook with big sobs. I held him close and stumbled down the rest of the steps, stunned.

A giant banner hung on the living-room wall that read: "Happy Last Day of Eleven, Macy!"

Mom hurried over, took Jack from me, and kissed me on the cheek. "I know you don't want to have your twelfth birthday until your dad is here, but the last day of being eleven is something to celebrate too!" She laughed at the look on my face.

"But I'm grounded and everything...," I mumbled.

"You certainly are, young lady! You're not going anywhere. That's why the party stays here."

Twee danced around me while Mom and Aunt Liv took turns patting, kissing, and shushing Jack. "Your mom is letting me sleep over, Macy! We've got tons of movies to watch and Chuck brought some of those insane chocolate mint mousse pies he sells. I know you love German chocolate the best, but—"

"Chocolate mint sounds—sounds great," I said, still feeling pretty blown away.

Aunt Liv scooped me into a big squeeze, lifting me off the floor, and then plopped me down. She eyeballed me. "I could just wring your skinny little neck for the scare you gave us the other day." She pecked me on the lips instead and then whispered into my ear. "We're all gonna be okay, sugar—promise!"

Switch cruised over wearing a giant Caffeine Nana's T-shirt that nearly hung to his knees. "Happy almost-birthday, kid," he said, grinning.

"So, you're *out*?" I asked stupidly, stating the obvious.

Chuck came up behind him, put one hand on his shoulder. "Just on loan," he clarified. "His probation officer was kind enough to give him a day pass. Your aunt Liv picked him up, and I'm taking him back later tonight."

"Just for the record,I am a lot safer driver than Mustang Sally over there," Switch said, jutting his chin toward Aunt Liv. "I wasn't sure I was going to see *my* next birthday, let alone yours this afternoon. I thought maybe your mom wanted me off her caseload!"

"She really likes you, Switch," I said. "I can tell. You wouldn't be here if she didn't."

His cheeks colored a bit, and he shrugged.

Aunt Liv threw some flirty looks at Chuck and then herded me into the kitchen, where an eye-boggling mountain of food, snacks, and desserts were assembled. Twee, Switch, and I packed our plates to capacity and carried them out to the living room. The grown-ups stayed in the kitchen, probably talking about the kitchen tile or the salsa recipe. Whatever weird things adults talk about.

"Man, I am so glad to see you, Twee!" I said, easing down next to her on the floor. "I have been dying to talk to you. I'm sorry I couldn't call you. I am grounded from everything."

She nudged me with her shoulder. "S'kay. Your mom called me. She didn't want me to think you were sore at me, or something. We'll catch up on everything later. It can wait." She gave me one of her famous full split-tooth smiles. I knew then she'd forgive me and she'd understand about everything. I sighed a deep sigh and took a big juicy bite of taco.

Switch sat on the floor and stretched his long legs out in front of him. He set his plate on his skateboard, which apparently could also be used as a dining-room table, if needed.

"How's the pizza, Tweetie?" he asked.

"TWEE!" we both screamed at him.

He tossed his head and gave us the official Switch the Slayer smile. He lowered his voice a little, his fork poised in midair. "So, Chuck told us about Mr. McDougall already being dead and all."

I nodded. "Yeah. It's so sad."

"I still don't get it," Twee said. "Chuck said Ginger was there when Mr. McDougall died, and she saw everything. . . ."

"It's complicated," I said. "I don't quite get it myself. It's like when kids still pretend to believe in Santa Claus or the tooth fairy, even when they know deep down that it's not true anymore. Her mind went to the pretend place. She pretended that Mr. McDougall was lost. Looking for him gave her something she could hope for each day when she woke up."

"So, she's not, like, crazy, is she?" Switch asked.

"No!" I said, shaking my head. "Mom says kids and older people are really lucky that they remember how to pretend."

"I used to pretend that my family wasn't poor," Switch said. "I told the kids at school the reason we didn't have a lot of food or any new clothes was because we were saving all our money to go live at Disneyland for a year."

"When I was in first grade," Twee confessed, "I used to pretend Mr. Hoang at the market was my real dad. I pretended so hard that I started to really believe it!"

"I remember that," I said. "You were always staring at him."

Jack toddled into the room just then, leading Aunt

Liv by the hand. She sat down on the ottoman near us. Deciding she looked like good lap material, Jack climbed aboard. She clasped her arms around him and buried her nose in his hair. "I swear one of these days I am going to kidnap this child. He smells like heaven."

I guffawed. "Yeah, but that's the good-smelling end of him. You should smell—"

Twee elbowed me. "Macy! We're trying to eat here!"

"Twee!" Aunt Liv exclaimed. "That reminds me. Any news from the hospital yet?"

"Not yet!" she said, and turned to me. "I didn't get a chance to tell you. Dad took Mom over to the hospital this morning. The babies are almost here— I can't wait!"

"You are going to be the world's best ever big sister, Twee," I said.

"Omigosh, did I tell you we get to name them? My parents couldn't agree on what to call them, so they decided to let us kids pick. Dad put all the names in a box, and once the twins get here, they are going to draw the winner." She gave a shiver of excitement and crossed all her fingers. "I hope they pick mine!"

"What did you choose, Twee?" Aunt Liv asked, gently unfurling Jack's fist from one of her dangly earrings.

"For the boy, Max. It's always been my favorite

boy name. And for the girl . . . ," she said, her cheeks getting a little pink.

"M-A-C-Y!" Switch spelled around a mouthful of taco.

She stared at him. "How did you know that?"

He rolled his eyes. "Total no-brainer."

"Really?" I grinned. "You put my name in?"

Twee put her arm around me and gave me a squeeze. "Of course I did. You're my best friend in the whole world. And don't you think 'Max' and 'Macy' sound so cute together?"

Switch got to his feet. "If you two are going to get all smoochy, I'm going for seconds. These are some serious vittles here."

We all watched him leave the room, and then Twee sighed. "I wish he didn't have to go back to jail after your party. It's not like any of this is his fault."

"I know; he's had it pretty tough. But at least juvie feels better to him than being in a foster home."

"I'm superglad your mom is his PO," Twee said. "I know she'll look out for him." She took a long swig of pink lemonade and then came up for air. "Hey! Maybe he could just come live with you guys. Your mom could be his foster parent!"

I choked on the nearly whole piece of pizza I was folding into my mouth.

Aunt Liv gave me some gentle pats on the back. "Easy there, girl. It wouldn't be the worst fate in the world. He's awfully cute! Don't you think he's cute, Macy?"

"And he could do all the chores you hate," Twee added. "He could mow the lawn and wash the car and—"

"And maybe watch this little fella," Aunt Liv said, lifting Jack's shirt to give him a big noisy raspberry on his stomach.

I tried to imagine having Switch around all the time. Well, he would certainly make an *interesting* older brother. Things wouldn't be boring, for sure.

Chuck came back into the room just then with Mom. He jingled his keys and smiled at me. "I hate that I have to leave, but I don't have anyone to cover the late-afternoon shift."

"That's okay!" I said. "I'm glad you came." I could hardly believe how glad I was, in fact.

"I have something for you before I go," he said. He raised his hand, as if he expected my protest. "Don't worry! It's not a birthday present." He reached deep into the big pocket in the side of his cargo pants and pulled out a package about the size of a small book. It was wrapped in brown paper, with an aqua-colored ribbon tied around it.

"Go ahead and open it, Macy," Mom said.

I always felt so shy opening gifts and cards in front of people, but I had to admit I was excited to see what it might be. My hands shook a bit as I tore the paper off. It was a photo of Nana's front window in a pretty silver frame.

"Oh! It's all repainted!" I gave Chuck a big smile.

Twee nudged me. "Look what it says, Macy."

"I know what it says," I told her. "I helped Chuck with it."

Twee took her finger and touched the photo. "Macy, *look*."

I caught my breath when my eyes finally saw it. I looked up at Chuck and then over at Mom. Then back at Chuck. "You changed it back," I said, my voice full of wonder.

The window read simply, at last, and once again, "Nana's."

"Honest?" I said, hardy able to believe it. "You're changing it for good?"

"Yes, I am," he said, and laughed when I lunged for him and wrapped my arms around his waist. I buried my head in his side a minute, afraid I might start bawling in front of everyone.

He gave me a squeeze and patted me on the back.

"I figured I'd never be able to get you girls to work there if I didn't change the name back to what it was."

"You're giving us jobs?" Twee asked, nearly shouting with excitement.

"Well, just Saturday mornings for now, if it's okay with your folks. But I'm going to need an assistant manager someday. Maybe even two if business picks up like I hope it will."

"It will," I said. "I bet you get a lot of Nana's old regulars back." I looked down at the photo again and traced my finger over the letters. "Thank you for this."

"Thank Ginger when you see her," he said. "She came and took the photo for you."

"How is she? Doing any better?" Aunt Liv asked.

He nodded. "We had a really good talk yesterday. I think she realized after the oven incident that she needs some help at home. She is not thrilled about it, but at least she didn't throw me out on the porch last night. That's progress."

"She let you use her wheels," Switch said. "She can't be too mad at you."

"I told her my van needed new brakes. I asked her if I could borrow her bike for a couple of weeks. I don't want her driving that thing right now." He shrugged. "We'll just take this a day at a time."

Aunt Liv sidled up to Chuck with Jack, who was conked out in her arms at this point. His cheeks were still red from all the excitement, but he was limp as old lettuce. "I wish you didn't have to leave so soon. I was just going to cut the cake."

A phone rang from the kitchen, and Twee nearly jumped out of her skin. "Maybe that's my dad about the babies!"

Mom dashed into the kitchen to get it, with Twee hot on her heels. She came back a moment later, holding it to her chest.

"Honey?" she said, looking at me. "You've got a phone call."

I looked back at her, surprised. Pretty much everyone I knew who would be calling me was in this room. Well, except for one person. Mom and I locked eyes, and she gave me a tiny smile.

I took the phone into the hallway where it was quieter, and closed the door. I leaned up against the wall and slid down to the floor. Slowly. I took a big, big breath in. Then exhaled.

"Hi, Dad," I said.

THE END

(Well, almost!)

Dear Mr. Jimenez,

The Seventh And Final Thing About Me: this is something I just discovered this summer. There is something about change that isn't completely terrible. Change still can hurt you something fierce and make you feel like you'll never get over something. But here's the thing—

Change never comes empty-handed. It brought me some amazing new friends.

And while I still think my mom is too snoopy and very stubborn, she and I have been having some pretty good talks about our family. But she still won't let me stay back a grade to be with Twee. So get ready, Mr. Jimenez, here I come!

Yours very sincerely,

Macy L. Hollinquest

ACKNOWLEDGMENTS

I am deeply thankful to Erin Murphy, my masterful agent, who challenged me to take a bracing breath and try, try again with this one.

And to Kristen Pettit, editor supreme, who is responsible for one of the best days of my life and surely my loudest "OMG" ever.

Mahalo to Jeanne Davis, who lent me her gorgeous home in Hawaii for three weeks, where I found the voice of this story again.

And to Leslie Harvey, who scooped me up and drove me 600 miles to Flag Buzz Coffeehouse in Flagstaff, where the book simply finished itself.

To Chuck Loring, one of the coolest, hunkiest, and finest men I have ever known. You made writing

Macy's Chuck such a breeze.

Finally, my gratitude to Dana, Kimmie Love, Lee, L'il Cookie, Carrie, Devon, Jean, and Bob—keepers of the dream, beloved friends.